Who Died In Here?

Who Died In Here?

25 Stories of Crimes & Bathrooms

Selected
by
Pat Dennis

First Edition

10 9 8 7 6 5 4

Typesetting by Wild Thoughts, Minneapolis, MN (612) 927-8018

Library of Congress Control Number: 2003098723

Cover Photo by Ben Kopilow, Fusion Photography. (www.fusionphotography.biz)

Who Died In Here? A collection of 25 mystery short stories of crimes and bathrooms.

ISBN: 0-9676344-2-3

Printed in the United States of America

For Gary Johnson & Lance Zarimba who laughed so hard at my punch line I had no choice but to turn it into a book.

Table Of Contents

Preface

The idea for *Who Died In Here?* sprouted at Mayhem in the Midlands, an annual convention for mystery authors and readers held in Omaha, Nebraska. I was telling my just-met-new-best-friends, Gary Johnson and Lance Zarimba, that an author friend of mine, Sharon Darby Hendry and her husband Bruce, keep a copy of my book "Hotdish To Die For" in the bathroom of their cabin in northern Wisconsin. Sharon says she can always tell when her guests are reading my book because she hears laughter coming from the room. And, as I told Gary and Lance, keeping any mystery book in a bathroom explains the age-old question—who died in here?

Gary and Lance howled with laughter. Lance said that should be the title of my next book and I left Omaha thinking seriously about his comment. I quickly realized it would be a great title for a collection of mystery short stories featuring crimes and bathrooms. But, I also knew I didn't want to write all of the stories myself and I had little interest in doing a book that could be dismissed as bathroom humor.

I am a devotee of the short story. It my favorite art form, and the mystery short story, my joy. I knew I wanted the stories in *Who Died In Here?* to be written by wonderful storytellers. I wanted the bathroom and crime to be secondary and the story itself to be primary. I also wanted the collection to range from hard-boiled to laugh-out-loud funny.

However, being Creative Director of a small independent publisher in Minnesota, I knew we could hardly offer authors either fame or fortune. Our only hope was that they too would embrace Penury's wacky promised payment of twenty-five bucks and an air freshener.

We received hundreds of submissions from around the world. We are delighted with the stories we have included in this edition of *Who Died In Here?* and hope you will be too.

R.T. Lawton

FLYING WITHOUT A PARACHUTE

Angel, pronounced AN-chell by all his close relatives, frequently remembered his warm days as a six-year old child. Times when he used to swipe one of his mother's large bath towels out of the linen closet. He'd tie the cloth around his neck like a huge red cape and run laughing from the house while his mother screamed at him to bring back her clean laundry.

"Come here you little trouble maker. You not thinking right. Joost wait 'til I catch you."

But he never waited and he never worried about getting his thinking right. He figured he was destined for bigger things in his young life and he was in a hurry to get there as he dashed out the front door. Then, with a long practiced running leap off the edge of his mother's front porch, he pretended to fly through the air like one of his comic book super heroes. Yeah, sure, the comedown was all too soon, yet still, in his youthful mind he believed he had actually suspended the laws of gravity and achieved the final freedom of flight.

It was in more recent days, as a thirty-year-old man hustling the streets with only the clothes on his back and an ancient, rust-pitted Owl Head revolver to work with, that he found himself now flying high on smack and coke. This wasn't the same as jumping off his mother's front porch and flying like his super heroes, but those sparkling little crystals in paper bindles did seem to maintain his ability to soar into the thin air of the upper regions and stay there longer than he had ever flown with that old red towel.

The flipside, one he didn't often share with friends, being that somehow the landings resulted in a lower elevation every time, as if the landing field were gradually sinking into the core of the earth. And, the sudden stop at the end of the ride came a lot harder now, with no bounce when he hit bottom. But, since flight was the main thing and he was stuck with one landing for every takeoff, he figured all he really needed in this life was more fuel to keep powering his launch back into the ethereal atmosphere.

And that's why, one lazy summer afternoon, Angel found himself standing once more on the front porch of James Lewis' old, three story, white, wood-frame house down on Troost Street. Angel was preparing to open the front door and go inside when he heard the high pitched scream of locked up rubber sliding on hot pavement. The sound seemed to be coming from directly behind him.

SCREEECH!

Turning quickly to the street, Angel watched two nondescript Ford Crown Victorias bounce over the curb and slide to a halt in James Lewis' front yard.

"Damn! Would you look at that," fell out of his mouth.

The car doors suddenly sprung open. Plainclothes detectives appeared with drawn guns and loud voices.

"Police!"

"Freeze!"

It just seemed common sense to Angel's mind, that with the front doorknob already open in hand, he should probably put the safety of the house walls between himself and the law. That and maybe keep on going, out the back door, across the alley, and possibly even several blocks down the road. It was better than doing time again.

SLAM!

He thrust the door closed behind him.

THUD!

He rammed the deadbolt into place.

Whirling around to make his exit through the ground floor apartment, he now found the way blocked by Lewis' brother.

"Where you think you going?"

"Through the house."

"Huh, uh. I own this house. Nobody goes through this inner door without my say so."

"But I'm a friend of James."

"More likely you mean one of his customers showing up here all hours of the night and day. Gotta get their morning pick-me-up and their evening come-on-down. That's how he afford the high rent he pays me."

"C'mon man, the cops are right outside the door."

"And that's the downside of renting that third floor apartment to my brother, James. I'm tired of the narc squad raiding my house all the time, so I'm adopting a new policy. From now on, I'm barricading my apartment door. Gonna remove myself as far as possible from any legal ramifications. You best be going on your way. Less you want them to catch you standing here flat-footed, of course. Bye now."

SLAM!

With the rear exit no longer available as an option and with the chilling shouts of man-hunters thundering up onto the front porch from the other side of the front door, Angel's brain flirted with the edge of panic. He couldn't seem to make up his mind even though he only had two clear choices left; head up the stairs or wait for the po-leece to nab him here in the foyer. And him being a felon in possession of a gun. The judge'd throw the Big Bitch at him, twenty to life in the slam. Not much to consider here. His feet took over on their own and moved him rapidly up the staircase to the second floor. The echoing pound of several other footsteps preceding him up the same stairs barely registered on his consciousness.

Arriving on the second floor just in time to see that particular apartment door slam shut and hear that deadbolt being thrown, Angel now noticed those same echoing footsteps that had preceded him from the ground floor to the second level had continued racing up to the third floor where James Lewis did his dealing.

From the depths of hell below Angel's feet, emanated the sounds of a crashed front door and the harrying cries of: "Federal agents" and "Search warrant." Angel looked down at the linoleum, then up at the ceiling. His feet, not wanting to spend too much time in meditation at a traumatic time like this, took over again and carried him up the last flight of stairs.

At the top of the landing, Angel stepped into the open loft which served as James Lewis' living room. Pausing briefly to swivel his head like he was watching the most important tennis match of his life, Angel took in the immediate upstairs situation.

To his left stood a kitchenette with a window way too small even for the skinny man currently trying to squeeze through the red curtained frame over the sink.

"Damn!"

That way was closed.

Casting his vision straight ahead through an open doorway, he caught the sight of James Lewis in the bathroom jamming two guns into his own oversized waistband while simultaneously trying to flush a large baggie of white powder down the white porcelain toilet. The partially opened window in this room was considerably larger than the one in the kitchen, but Angel wasn't sure he could get past Lewis' obese body in such a small room.

Glancing quickly to his right, Angel caught the sound of breaking glass and observed two males in the process of bailing out of the bedroom window which would then drop them down on top of the porch roof in the front of the house where they obviously hoped to make a successful departure. Angel was pretty sure the po-leece would leave a man out front like they always did to catch any one trying to exit in that direction. At least this way, the cop's attention would be drawn to the front of the house.

Since all the other available windows of any size were being utilized by other escapees, Angel grabbed up a nearby wooden chair and advanced toward the bathroom.

"Get out of my way, James. I'm coming through."

"Forget you, man. I gotta get rid of this dope and the toilet's plugging up. Find another way out. I got my own troubles."

"Ain't got time for this. I'm desperate here, and I'm warning you to move."

"Screw you," and Lewis went back to his flushing.

Angel moved the wooden chair over to his left hand and drew out the old Owl Head revolver with his right. He pointed the gun into the bathroom.

"Last chance."

Lewis ignored him.

Discharging all five shots that were nestled in the cylinder, Angel rushed through the doorway. He tossed the empty Owl Head into the bathtub, then swung the chair up over his head with both hands. With a forward motion he threw the chair toward the window.

WHOOOOSH!

The chair passed quietly through the already opened bottom window frame, arced gracefully over the single car driveway on the south side of the house and landed in the soft green grass of the neighbor's yard.

Adrenaline pumping to the max and without further hesitation, Angel took a running start and stepped up on Lewis' soft, squishy back which was now hunched motionless across the overflowing toilet. With a strong kickoff, Angel launched himself head first through the open window to follow the flight of the wooden chair.

Sailing through the open frame, the toe of his right shoe caught briefly on the inside bottom of the window ledge, but it was enough. As he saw the rapidly approaching gray cement of the driveway, Angel wished he once again had his old red cape to help him fly as it used to do in his super hero youth.

One landing coming up.

R.T. Lawton is a retired federal lawman with 38 published short stories, which includes five in Alfred Hitchcock's Mystery Magazine. He is an active member of the Mystery Writers of America and the Short Mystery Fiction Society.

NOTHING GOOD EVER CAME OF A BAD HAIR DAY

Brandi, my hairdresser, turned me away from the mirror when she cut my hair that morning. I didn't mind. It was tough enough to rehearse my closing arguments, while remembering to punctuate her running commentary on Real Life—on Survivor, that is—with an occasional "Uh-huh," without any other distractions. I put my remarks to her on autopilot and just tuned out everything but the words scrolling through my mind, knowing whatever happened that day would govern the rest of my life.

Then she turned me back to the mirror.

"But—but—" I sputtered. "That's not my usual look."

"I thought you needed some fun in your life. This is the real you, anyway."

The real me? Maybe if I had a Multiple Personality Disorder.

"I suppose I can pat it down," I said. *Please*, tell me I could.

"You weren't paying attention, silly," Brandi said. "Why did you think I put in those perm rods except to make it spring up like that? This is the latest look according to all the magazines. Everyone is wearing it."

Everyone? I couldn't say. There weren't a lot of circus clowns working at Slaughter, Cohen, Rather, Word &

Dragger—or as I thought of it, SCREWED—where I faced my absolute last chance at making partner, before being shunted off onto the eternal loser track. Let's face it, I was out of my league at SCREWED, a law firm where the quota for billable hours exceeded the hours in a week, even if sleep were not an option, and where back-stabbing had become a gold-medal event. I'd been faking my way through all along, but now I was down to the wire.

And I had to face that challenge with this hairdo. The top was a bird's nest, in a tornado. The sides, a Marine Corp buzz. It curled where it should have been straight, and stuck out rigidly where it should have turned under. The ends twinkled iridescently in artificial light.

Don't try telling me everyone isn't really superficial, deep down. Who would listen to anything I said when I looked like this? My client's fate, and more importantly—mine— rested on people who would judge me by my looks.

Well, maybe it wasn't that bad. I watched for the reaction of the salon receptionist when she extracted the tariff they charged for the unexpected perm. She couldn't say enough positive things about the change in my appearance. To carry that off so well, she either had to mean it—or she was in cahoots with the hairdressers. I wasn't so paranoid as to think they had a conspiracy going against their clients.

When the real world vote came in at the courthouse, I realized I may have rushed to judgment on that conspiracy-idea. The judge covered his face with his hands to hide his laughter, while his robes quivered like Jell-O. The spectators weren't as restrained; they shouted increasingly more disgusting metaphors for my hairdo throughout the remainder of the trial. My new look even brought a smile to my client's lips, the only part that cheered me, as I suspected it would be the last thing he had to smile about for a long time.

While waiting in the corridor for the inevitable thumbs down from the jury, I kept hearing my name murmured, followed by raucous laughter that echoed against the marble halls. I knew then that Brandi would have to pay.

It took nearly a week to put my scheme into motion. Fortunately, none of my cases came to trial during that time, so I let the work slide. First stop, the cutlery store. I should bring as much persuasive aplomb to my juries as I did to the guy behind the counter there.

He squinted at me. "You want me to do what? I don't sell no trick scissors, you know."

With a face straighter than my ends, I repeated my demand until he finally agreed.

I also had to enlist the unwitting help of my assistant, Nora. Fortunately, she so wanted to walk in my footsteps there at SCREWED—until I happened into this hair doo-doo—that she went to Brandi for her haircuts, too.

"I don't know," Nora said when I showed her my purchase from the cutlery store. "You want me to replace Brandi's shears with this pair when she isn't looking? Why would you buy your hairdresser new scissors?"

"Don't be a doofus, Nora. So I can stay on her good side, of course." As if leaving hefty tips, never uttering a peep of reproach when she kept me waiting long enough to grow another ring around my trunk, and dropping a bigger bundle on designer hair products than I put into my pension plan each year—wouldn't be enough to win her over.

"You know what my schedule's like. It's hard for me to find time to get my hair done, and it's important that I always look my best." I actually delivered that last line without flinching, that's how determined I was. "I want her to feel so grateful, she'll always fit me in."

Nora was actually buying it. I could tell by the sly look that stole over her face. Her schedule was even less flexible than mine, since I usually made her work through lunch. She was probably thinking that if she gave up food entirely, she might save enough to buy something that would win Brandi's gratitude, too.

"But if I sneak it into her drawer, how will she know it's from you? When will you tell her?" Nora asked.

"Later," I said. *Much* later.

Nora carried out her mission. I knew that because, judging by appearances, she was the first client to benefit from those shears. The guy in the cutlery store was a genius. My plan worked even better than I imagined.

And yet, it backfired.

"Do you like it?" Nora asked, beaming proudly.

Like it? It looked as if a blind man took a weed-whacker into a spaghetti factory.

"It's the latest thing, according to Brandi. All the other stylists can't wait to give it to their clients, too."

So there really was a conspiracy of chatter in those places. I should have known no hairdresser would ever admit to a mistake. It's always *your* fault because you used the wrong gel — even if it was the one they twisted your arm to buy last month. They always act like they intended to create that monstrosity, even that you asked for it. I couldn't get to Brandi through her clients, I realized. The system was designed to cover their mistakes.

She could only be reached through her own appearance.

Plan Two began the next day. I staked out Brandi's station from the manicurist's table. Oh, sure, I maxed out my credit card paying for all the services I charged during my lengthy stay there, and, with all the noxious chemicals I breathed, probably relinquished my ability to bear children as well. But it was worth it.

I knew if I waited long enough, there would come a time when all of Brandi's clients would either be under the hot lights with enough foil in their hair to receive transmissions from Saturn, or waiting in the lobby till she was good-and-ready—and she would wander off to call the latest in a long line of men who could actually claim a low enough IQ to rival hers. Sometimes it scared me how many of those there were. When she did, I crept to her station and swiped her spare set of keys.

That afternoon I needed to write a brief for one of my cases, but I couldn't wait to carry out my plan. I put Nora on it and swore her to secrecy, in case the partners checked on me. I'd long suspected she knew more about legal crap than I did, anyway.

I parked my car across from Brandi's apartment at the usual start of my work day—six o'clock—and waited till she put in an appearance at the dawn of hers—ten or eleven. I slid down in the seat when she drove past, so that hairdo didn't give me away. Then I nonchalantly approached her apartment door.

I'd taken the precaution of dressing like a cleaning lady in case I ran into anyone. Good cover, with the household products I carried. My disguise worked. As I passed one of Brandi's neighbors, I heard her mutter, "A maid? Brandi must be doing well."

Of course, she was, the lying bitch. But her days were numbered.

I overcame the desire to snoop through Brandi's place, to see what all my money bought, and just went right to work in the bathroom. It gave me endless satisfaction to flush her hoity-toity hair products down the toilet. I refilled the bottles with a solution of Lava soap and acetone, the latter idea having come to me in a flash during my second pedicure. The odor still gave it away, so I topped off each container with a splash from the pricey bottle of Calvin Klein's *Good Smell Stuff*, which I found on the vanity.

Then all I had to do was wait for my revenge to pan out.

It didn't take long. You'd think her hair would have taken more abuse. When I returned for my follow-up chop, I could barely contain my glee when I saw how dry and flyaway Brandi's long auburn locks had become. She didn't have split ends, but shattered shafts! I went in for the kill.

"Gee, Brandi, what are you using on your hair?"

She tried to maintain the facade. "What do you mean? The same products I always use, of course. I wouldn't take chances with my hair."

"They're sure not working for you. How can I trust my hair to someone who can't handle her own?"

Yes! My doubts nearly reduced her to tears.

Till one of her co-conspirators from a neighboring station jumped in. "Oh, she just got a bad batch of something. She should get rid of her shampoo and start fresh. With the deep discounts we get, it's no biggie, anyway."

Nooo! I'd come so close to securing my revenge, only to have it snatched away. Once she switched to a new shampoo, the bounce in her hair would return. But she hadn't paid a big enough price yet for what she did to me. Well, I still had her keys. I would just have to keep at it for as long as it took to break her.

I made destroying Brandi's life my job. Fortunately, Nora was a real brick about the office work I kept missing. I adulterated every hair care product Brandi brought into that apartment.

Payback finally came. As Brandi's hair began falling out, so did the loyalty of her clients. She was reduced to taking—yes—walk-ins. And finally, the ultimate disgrace—a second job at Butchercuts. Ah, the humiliation.

It should have been enough for me. It would have been, only Nora informed me the firm was so impressed with her efforts during my repeated absences, they were sending her to law school! Can you believe the ingratitude? With my life going down the toilet as surely as Brandi's hair care products, I knew I'd never be satisfied with anything less than the total destruction of the person who set it all in motion.

Brandi would have to die.

I'd love to describe the elaborate scheme I brought to her

murder, but the truth is, people were starting to talk about how often that maid came to clean her apartment. Some of them must have noticed what a mess it remained after she left, too. I was terrified one of them would call the cops. Anyway, why change a winning formula? The ring I always saw around her bathtub, which I wasn't about to clean, told me how often she soaked. So I just concocted a new bubble bath for her. It wasn't much different from her usual stuff, with the exception of a slight addition of caustic lime.

Well, maybe I went a bit heavy on the active ingredient. The stuff worked so effectively, there wasn't much left apart from some bones in the tub when I went back into her bathroom to remove the evidence. I kept those bones as souvenirs, and they still give me a warm glow when I look at them. If I thought she'd understand the warning, I'd send them to Nora.

I left the law after that. Well, yeah, the partners did inform me that I was now so far off even the associate track at SCREWED, about all I could aspire to was the janitor track. Yet I prefer to think I simply chose a higher calling. I'm in the justice game now, and if you think that's the same as the law and that I'm just splitting hairs here—heh, heh—you've never worked in a law office.

I haven't entered a salon since Brandi's death. That conspiracy will never again enslave me. I cut my own hair now, with garden shears, in the kitchen, without a mirror. I clean my locks and my laundry with the same suds. I'm free, I tell you—free. Oh, sure, they're all bad hair days now, but who cares? I knew I had finally rid myself of the monkey on my back when I could no longer remember the last time I secretly yearned to look like Jennifer Aniston.

I have a calling now. I'm devoting my life to eliminating every soul-sucking salon on the face of the earth, starting with the really chi-chi ones where you have to give an extra tip to a shampoo girl or you look cheap.

It was slow work, getting rid of one hairdresser at a time,

but satisfying. I was making progress, too. If you don't believe me, check out the prices now that there's a shortage of stylists. Just goes to show what one twisted individual can accomplish when she follows her dream.

I also make my services available to others on occasion, when I believe their cause is just and their cut demands it. I don't know how people learn my phone number, but when they need it, it just seems to come to them. Maybe it floats in on a whisper when they've been under the dryer so long their brains have melted. Or it flashes before their eyes in strange hues when someone reads their color formula wrong. However they find me, I take on their cause with the same relish as I did my own.

I'd like to share it with you. It's not just my telephone number, it's my motto. Say it to yourself so you'll remember it if you ever need it. If you make it your motto, too, I guarantee you'll need it. It's:

1-800-I-DON'T NEED-NO-STINKING-
CONDITIONER

Remember: If you don't look good, my work is done.

Kris Neri writes the wacky and sassy Agatha, Anthony and Macavity Award-nominated Tracy Eaton mysteries, REVENGE OF THE GYPSY QUEEN and DEM BONES (Worldwide Mystery). She has also published fifty short stories, two of which won the Derringer Award for Best Short Story. She teaches crime writing for the prestigious Writers' Program of the UCLA Extension School. (www.krisneri.com)

HARD WORKING RED

Red Fitzpatrick was always a hard worker. The product of a poor home, at the age of eight he helped with the family finances by stealing newspapers from the front porches of rich neighbors and selling them downtown on the street corner.

His mother wanted to fulfill her Irish Catholic obligation to the church by encouraging Red to enter the priesthood. But Red was far too interested in making a buck to be satisfied counting the church poor box. Red Fitzpatrick was going places.

Red grasped early on that there was a great deal of money to be made in doing the things the Harvard boys felt they were too good for. Like, plumbing for example.

So, out of high school Red apprenticed as a plumber. He was serious about his work. In fact, he became known quickly as the "go to" guy—no job was too difficult, no job beneath him. Red Fitzpatrick wasn't afraid to get his hands dirty.

Red spent five years as an apprentice, and easily passed his journeyman exam, finally becoming a master plumber with the largest contractor in town, Acme.

Then Red decided to take business classes at the local community college, and in two years earned his associates degree. It wasn't long before he not only worked as a plumber for Acme, but also stayed nights and worked weekends doing the bookkeeping.

During a particularly bad economic turndown Red noticed Acme was heading towards a nasty cash flow period. Shortly after, at the age of 31, he bought out Acme, and it became *Fitzpatrick Plumbing and Contracting*. Some later said the coincidence was curious, Red being the bookkeeper, and then buying the business. But Red paid no attention to such talk from jealous minds.

His business in place, Red decided to build a family.

Sophia Mengoni was the prettiest girl in high school; a blonde haired Northern Italian beauty, the granddaughter of the head of the notorious Mengoni crime family, Red was so far beneath Sophia's radar that in high school she didn't even bother mocking him. She was too busy dating boys like Johnny Simone, a slick, obnoxious skirt chaser who used to throw beer bottles at Red and was now an electrician with ties to the mob, and possibly the only person in the world whom Red Fitzpatrick actually hated.

After graduation, Sophia and Johnny were engaged for a time. But then she broke off the engagement. By day, she went through life cutting and washing hair at the Tres Fabu Hair Salon, and by night, dated a never-ending collection of losers.

When her grandfather was found dead in the trunk of his Cadillac, Red took the opportunity to go to Nicky Mengoni's funeral hoping to get a look at the dead mobster's granddaughter. But Sophia was nowhere to be seen. It then became clear to Red that she had cut herself off from her family, and he realized she wanted no part of the life her grandfather led, or of guys like Johnny Simone. Red saw an opening, and he went for it.

Over the next several months he pursued Sophia with the same careful planning with which he had done everything in his life. He even hired a private detective to follow her. He discovered what kind of flowers she liked, wine she drank, music she listened to, then sent her bouquets of her favorite flowers, bottles of her favorite wine, albums of her favorite bands. With each of these deliveries he enclosed a note that simply said, "From Someone Who Understands."

Finally, after weeks of this, he waited outside the salon for her. As she came out from her day's work, she had a bouquet of *his* flowers in her hand, and he noticed she was smiling as she read the card!

He introduced himself and her smile turned to a puzzled expression. She remembered him, she said. Then, terrified she would laugh at him, he told her that *he* was the person who understood. He was her secret admirer. He poured his heart out to her, and an odd thing happened: she didn't laugh at all. Sophia Mengoni, self-exiled from her family and forced to work for a living, knew a gravy train when she saw it, and she willingly climbed aboard. They were married six months later.

Red had almost everything he had ever wanted. Almost. It was time to go to work on some kids.

But two years went by, and there weren't any kids. Of course, in order to have youngsters one would actually have to have sex with the wife. And *his* wife didn't seem too keen on that idea. To his dismay, he'd have to get her pretty much filled with her favorite wine (which he knew from pre-marital research) to make that happen, and the last time they shared the joys of the marriage bed occurred several months earlier.

Maybe she needed some space. Maybe the night courses she was taking would give her something to do, make her feel better about herself, and then she'd feel differently about him and about having children. Maybe it would.

See, Red wasn't one to become easily discouraged. He worked too hard for everything he had in his life to be a quitter. And he was certain he would find a solution to his current domestic problem if he just put his mind to it.

This was the exact thing Red was wrestling with as he

worked on finishing up a bathroom installation at a job site in a new development outside of town. Red liked new construction–the pipe fitting, putting in new fixtures. It wasn't like working in someone's home with the owner hovering over you and blabbing in your ear all the time. With new construction you had time to think.

Unfortunately, because of a scheduling mix up and a job completion deadline, the general contractor had called Red to the site on the very same day as the electrician, and much to his discomfort Red found himself working side by side in a small bathroom with the only man he hated in the world: *Johnny Simone.*

Johnny turned to his apprentice who was wiring the light switch on the bathroom wall. "Hey Charley. Do you smell somethin'?"

Charlie turned from his wiring, giggled, but said nothing. Red was setting the commode in place, while Johnny was working on the outlet to the left of the basin, near the toilet tank. It was cramped quarters, and Johnny's loud mouth didn't help matters any.

"Yeah, I definitely smell something," he repeated. Then, looking down at Red, he exclaimed in mock surprise, "oh— I see what it is—it's a plumber!" whereupon his apprentice blurted out a laugh that sounded like it was coming from a sixth grade school girl.

Red said nothing, however. He just kept to his work. He hated Johnny Simone, and he refused to give him the time of day.

"Yeah, you made the right choice Charley to apprentice in electrics. Hey Red, did you know that Charley here was gonna apprentice as a plumber? Ain't that right, Charley?"

"That's right," the apprentice parroted back.

"Too smart for it though. Yeah, the only thing plumbers know is that Friday is payday and that it all flows downhill!"

This witticism was rewarded once again by another annoying laugh by Charley, and this time Johnny joined him in appreciation of his own comedy.

Red kept his head down, busy with his work. The room was so close he could smell the Jim Crow on Johnny's breath. God, how he hated him.

"You know Charley, I read in the paper today there was this bum in New York City, and he took a leak over the edge of the subway platform, and he hit the electrified third rail, and, zap! Electrocuted himself." Charley clucked in amazement. "Yep. They found out afterwards the bum was a plumber; he was trying to get into electrics!"

With that, they both collapsed in laughter. But once again, Red held his tongue.

Johnny, seeing these initial attempts at baiting were not getting the desired rise out of Red, decided to change his tactics.

"Well Charley, at least we don't smell like a sewer when we go home to our wives at night."

Red dropped his pipe wrench, and Johnny saw that as an encouraging sign to pursue this line of attack.

"Speaking of wives, Charley, did you know I used to be engaged to Red's missus?"

Charlie finished wiring and turned the light switch to test the circuit, lighting the overhead. "Really?"

"Oh yeah. Sophia and me were quite an item. She used to be able to do this thing with her legs; she still do that, Red?"

Red gripped his pipe wrench until his knuckles were white. He looked up at Johnny Simone with his jet-black oily hair and thought seriously of parting it down the middle by bashing his brains in.

But then Red's eyes fell on the outlet Johnny was wiring, and he smiled.

He told Johnny he thought he was making a mistake with that outlet. See, he said, all outlets in bathrooms have to be special G.F.I. outlets; they have a built-in circuit breaker that would sense whether or not, say, your hands were wet—as they could very well be in a bathroom. If they were, why, the circuit would trip and you wouldn't be electrocuted. But Johnny was putting in a regular outlet. That certainly wasn't up to code, Red told him, and he was certain it wouldn't pass inspection.

Johnny turned white, and Charley got real quiet. Because of course, Red was right; Johnny had a few too many drinks that morning, and he was putting in the wrong outlet.

"Hey Methane Man, why don't you mind your own damn business," Johnny blurted, and Red thought that "Methane Man" was pretty clever for a guy as stupid as Johnny was. "I knew about the switch; I don't have one on me and was gonna replace it out after lunch, that's all." Then, not willing to let Red have the last laugh, he moved in with his heavy artillery.

"But you probably know all about G.F.I. switches, since you have one next to your bathtub. That way Sophia can take those long soapy bubble baths and listen to the radio." He smirked and winked at Charley. "That's what she does instead of sleeping with you, doesn't she, Red?"

Red grabbed Johnny's shirt and was about to break his head open like a watermelon, when Charley stepped in and pulled them apart.

"Whoa, fellahs. It's getting a little, uh, hot in here. Maybe we oughta break for lunch Johnny. Whatta ya say?"

Johnny and Red stood looking each other eye to eye, and in that moment something passed between them and Red knew: *Johnny was sleeping with his wife.*

It made sense. Sophia's "night classes?" He never saw any books, and she was vague about what she was studying. Obviously, she was studying Johnny Simone. And Red could see it on Johnny's face: his expression said it all. How could he have missed it?

Johnny pulled away from Red and backed up a step. "Yeah, okay. Lunch. How about it, Red, wanna beer? I've got a cooler in the truck."

Red told him he'd be working through lunch. He had a

job to do.

But Red's head was swimming. As he heard the laughter from Johnny's truck outside, he was all but determined to walk out there and beat him to death with his wrench. The miserable scum that used to flick cigarette butts at him in high school was now screwing his wife, and Red was going to kill him. It didn't matter if he went to prison and lost everything he had worked so hard for, he wouldn't let this nothing make a fool of him.

And he wasn't even angry with Sophia. You see, he still loved her, and in Red's mind she was being sucked back into her old life by this predator, Johnny Simone. It was the life she had rejected and the life he had taken her away from, and Johnny Simone was preying on her like a coyote preys on a lost kitten. So, Red was going to kill him, and it may as well be now; then things would be okay with Sophia again. Once again, Red would rescue her.

He grabbed his pipe wrench and stood up to go outside to Johnny's van.

But then Red's eyes fell on the half finished unprotected outlet next to the toilet tank, hanging there where Johnny had left it. Red looked down and flushed the commode he had just installed. He looked again at the outlet, inches away. Johnny was out in his truck having beers. Having a great many beers.

Red decided: it would be nothing, nothing at all to run a small wire from that unprotected, hot outlet into the top of the toilet tank and right down into the water. It could easily be done. Soon nature would have its way with Johnny's bladder, and soon he'd be running in here to use these very facilities. And he'd be way too much in the bag to notice.

Oh yes. It would be all *too* easy.

Sophia sat very, very still, a blank, horrified expression on her face. Red apologized again for being late; the police had wanted him to make a statement, and he had to stay. He was as surprised as Charley was that poor old Johnny could have electrocuted himself in that bathroom. It was certainly baffling; Red had been the first to find him, the first to hear the scream. Charley was still in the truck. Yep, Red found him dead on the floor, his Johnson hanging out of his unzipped pants. Of course, Red did not mention, either to the police or to Sophia, that while he was there, smiling down at Johnny's dead body and crispy manhood, that he carefully disconnected a small wire from the outlet and removed it from the toilet tank.

So the police were baffled; Johnny Simone must have been so drunk (his blood alcohol level was off the charts) that he *somehow* electrocuted himself. Such a waste, Red said to his wife, as a tear ran down her cheek.

That night he had her. And six months later, their first child was born. Red named him John and pretended that the math made sense.

For years afterward people remarked on John's jet-black hair, Red's carrot top, and the fact that Sophia was blonde.

And Red would just smile. He had everything he always wanted in the world.

He had worked hard for it.

Thomas Bray has acted on stage, in films and television, and written and produced for such TV shows as *Designing Women*, *Now & Again* and *Nash Bridges*. Now approaching his dotage, he has turned to writing fiction as an excuse to keep buying the latest computer. Thom lives in Portland, Oregon. (www.thom-bray.com)

JUST PASSIN' THROUGH

"Ma, come quick! Some city man's up and died in the outhouse!"

Arling Whitaker paused, the top button of her gingham dress pinched between her fingers. She stared at her son then finished buttoning. "Lavon, it's too early in the morning for your nonsense."

Lavon's face fell the way it did those rare times he was unfairly accused. "But, Ma, it's true! Come see."

Arling sighed. "Well, I was heading that way, anyhow." Lavon raced out of the house, leapt off the wooden porch, and tore across the small field the Whitakers called their lawn. He clattered over the two planks bridging the stream and pulled up at the white outhouse, shifting his weight back and forth. Arling wondered if it was from excitement or needing to pee.

She caught up with the boy, wiping sweat from her forehead with the back of her hand. It was going to be another hot day, for sure. "Now what's this about?"

Lavon pointed to the closed door with its crescent moon vent. "Go on, look!"

"Mmm hmm." Arling pulled the door open warily, remembering last summer when she found a box of baby garter snakes Lavon had hidden inside. She'd been constipated for a month after that.

The door creaked open; the familiar pungent smell rushed over her in its escape. She peered inside.

"Well, Lord have mercy!" she whispered.

Sitting on the seat plain as day was a man, probably in his late seventies, dressed in a black three-piece suit. His chin rested on his chest; his hands lay in his lap, palms up. He looked asleep.

"Sir?" Arling said. He didn't move.

She stepped inside, peered more closely at him, poked him gently on the shoulder.

"Is he really dead, Ma?"

Arling nodded. "He sure enough is that."

"Wow! Who is he? Ever seen him before? Was he shot?"

Arling stepped back out into the morning sunlight. She blinked thoughtfully at the corpse, her fingers idly tugging at the single hair that grew from a small mole on her chin. "It don't make no sense. Why in tarnation would a city man come all the way down into Happy Holler just to up and die in someone's outhouse?"

"I bet the sheriff was chasing him and he got shot and ran in here and died!"

Arling's eyes narrowed. "Now, now, let's just figure on this a bit." She looked toward the road. "You can bet dollars to doughnuts he didn't *walk* all the way down here—his shoes look like they was just polished. No siree Bob, he drove, or someone drove him."

Lavon looked crestfallen, but returned with a new theory, backed up with his twelve-year-old enthusiasm. "I bet he's a crook, maybe from up in Chicago, and someone kilt him to keep him from talking to anyone!"

Arling smiled and rubbed her son's bristly head. "Well now, that's just possible, though I ain't sure they'd drive him three hundred mile just to kill him. Let's us see if we can come up with another idea, just in case that one don't pan out."

Lavon shrugged as though thinking that was unlikely but willing to humor his mom.

Arling bent down and gently turned over one of the man's feet. "See here? Look at them scuffs on the back of his shoes. He was drug into this outhouse, no doubt about it."

Lavon's eyes widened.

"And it had to happen before that big storm come through last night; otherwise, his shoes'd be all muddy."

"Wow! What else, Ma?"

Arling puffed up her cheeks, blew out a long breath, and went back to stroking her chin hair. "But if someone kilt him, why'd they go to all the trouble to prop him up in here, pretty as a picture, knowing we'd find him first thing? Seems like they'da just dumped him off in a ditch somewheres."

"It's like they wanted him found."

Arling smiled and nodded. "Right as rain, son. And you know what else? I'm thinking maybe this poor feller wasn't murdered. Ain't no blood or nothing, no sign of a struggle. And don't he look peaceful?"

Lavon re-examined the dead man, then nodded. "Yeah, Ma, he does. He reminds me of Grandpa, at the funeral."

A brief pain flared in Arling's heart. "Yes, child, he does at that." She took a deep breath to pull herself back to the moment. "Well, your Pa took the car up to the churchyard this morning. Seems to me he mighta noticed a dead man in the outhouse before he left. Unless . . ." She turned and squinted at the wilted sunflowers growing along the side of the house. "I guess now I know why them flowers ain't do-ing no better."

"What are we gonna do, Ma?"

"First things first." Arling reached into the outhouse and tore off a strip of toilet paper, then closed the door and dropped the nail-hook into the eye-screw. Stepping behind a large tree, she said, "You just look the other way. I ain't about to go moving a dead man just 'cause I got to pee."

Back at the kitchen sink, they took turns working the pump

handle while the other washed their hands under the cool water splashing from the spout. "I don't like the idea of leaving that poor soul in there all day," Arling said. "Let's us walk over to the Johnson's. Emma Mae's always bragging about that telephone they got put in. We'll call the sheriff and let him figure it out."

The Johnson farm lay a mile down the road. The mother and son walked along the gravel path in the sunshine, listening to the bobwhites and whippoorwills, Arling enjoying the scents of late spring, Lavon throwing rocks at fence posts. After a half-hour, they stepped onto a wooden porch much like their own and knocked on their neighbor's screen door.

A pimply faced young man of about twenty pushed the door open. "Hey, Mizz Whitaker. Lavon."

"Morning, Vernon. Mind if we use your telephone?"

"Sure, c'mon in. Y'all want some lemonade? It's hotter'n the devil's griddle out there already."

"That'd be fine, thank you."

Arling stopped on the threshold and narrowed her eyes at the young man. "Vernon?" she said in a slow, accusing tone.

He suddenly looked like he'd been caught stealing their apples again. "Yes, Ma'am?"

"You don't seem particular surprised to see us here, seven in the morning, asking to use your telephone."

"Uh—"

Arling nodded. "Uh" was Vernon's usual comeback when he was in trouble. "I see. Let's us go out on the porch for a spell."

Vernon blushed like an overripe strawberry and stepped outside with them.

"Vernon, was you out last night? Maybe up to the dance?"

Vernon cocked his lower jaw to one side, drew a circle on the wooden planks with his toe. "Uh, yeah."

"And what time d'you reckon you got home?"

"I dunno. 'Bout midnight, just before the storm hit."

Arling looked down at her son; Lavon grinned back at

her. "You want to tell me about the car, or should I call your ma out here so's you can explain it to *her*?"

Vernon's eyes swelled like a startled calf's. "Don't do that, Mizz Whitaker! I'll tell ya what happened." He cast a glance at the screen door and lowered his voice.

"I was driving back home last night, and I saw some fancy car pulled off the side of the road, not a stone's throw from your place. 'Well,' says I, 'that don't seem quite right.' The engine was running, but I couldn't see nobody inside. I pulled over an' got out with a tire iron and walked up to it. That's when I seen the hose."

"Hose?" Lavon asked.

Vernon nodded. "Yeah, there was a hose running from the exhaust pipe up through one of the windows. I saw a man sleeping in the back seat. Well, not asleep." He paused. "The doors was unlocked. I opened it up—it was a four-door— and let the fumes all out, then pulled that ol' boy out. I shook him, but he was dead as a door-nail."

Arling nodded. "Nice car, I reckon?"

Vernon looked up, eyes bright. "Hell yeah—er, sorry, Ma'am. Heck yeah, it was a beaut! Anyway, I figgered he wasn't gonna need it no more, so I drug him up to your out- house, figger'n you'd find him first thing this morning and drive him up to the sheriff's." He paused. "But then when you'ns showed up knocking and asking about the phone, I figgered it was because of that."

Arling shook her head. "Vernon Cale Johnson! I can't believe you was just gonna steal that man's car! What about his family, his wife and kids?"

Vernon shook his head. "He ain't got none. Hell—I mean, heck, Mizz Whitaker, I wouldn't steal, 'specially not from a widow. Here, read this." He pulled a wadded paper from his overalls pocket and thrust it into Arling's hand. She uncrinkled it and read:

I have a plot in the Lord's Embrace graveyard over in Union County. Put me there next to my wife, Jenny. She died four years ago. Our only child's already passed on, so you don't need to worry about that, or any other family, either. I already took care of what affairs I had left. I'm dying of cancer, and I just don't have the courage to go through what my Jenny did. She always was the brave one.

God bless you.

Arling read the note twice, then let Lavon read it and handed it back to Vernon.

"I wonder what brung him down here?" Lavon asked.

Arling shrugged. "He was an old man; he coulda growed up and moved out of these parts before I was ever born." She shook her head. "Or maybe he was only passing through. Hard knowing, I reckon. Where'd you put his car, Vernon?"

"Around behind the barn. I was trying to figger a way to tell mom how I got it. Maybe won it in a raffle or something."

Arling smiled. "You never was the shiniest apple in the bushel, Vernon." She shook her head. "And boy, you ain't got the sense God gave a goose—but I appreciate you being willing to stop in the middle of the night to watch out for us—and with no more'n a tire iron."

Vernon's eyes brightened, but not for long.

"Now you take that fancy car up to the sheriff's and tell him what happened. He'll give you a good lecture, you can be sure of that. You listen to him, too, you hear?"

Vernon sighed and nodded.

"Can I go with him, Ma?"

"That'd be fine. I'm proud of you too, Lavon. You was brave today. Real brave."

Lavon beamed. Vernon pulled a set of keys from his pocket. "I reckon you're right. You want a ride back to your place, Mizz Whitaker?"

Arling shook her head, watching some swallowtail butterflies dancing over honeysuckle blossoms along the road. "It's a right fine day for a walk."

Vernon grinned down at Lavon. "Race ya to the barn!"

And the two took off, a blur of elbows, knees, and sneakers streaking across the field, one bursting toward adulthood, one already there but not sure what to do about it. Arling watched them, smiling to herself.

When she got home, Arling stopped at the outhouse once more. She opened the door and looked at the peaceful man at rest inside.

"You know, stranger, I guess we're all just passing through, in our own way; it seems a shame to go and cut the trip short. If you'd a just come up to the house we'd have invited you in, gave you a good meal and some good company. Maybe you'da changed your mind. Maybe you'd still be here, enjoying this beautiful day like the rest of us."

She sighed. "Then again, maybe not. I'll go say a prayer for you, and I'll ask God to have mercy on your soul. I think He will, since it don't seem like he showed you much while you was down here."

She closed the door.

———————

Terry Burlison grew up amidst the cornfields of Indiana, not escaping until age 23. He worked as a space shuttle mission controller for NASA, for Boeing Aerospace Company, and is currently a consultant for any aerospace company whose checks don't bounce. He also has his own business developing and publishing music and game software, and spends his idle time playing guitar for his wife and two daughters, or writing— mostly humor articles about his annual surgeries. (www.sixstring.com/ terryburlison)

Michael Giorgio

NOBODY CARES

If Arley Putch's insulin delivery had been on time for a change, he wouldn't have witnessed the accident. But as usual, the Free Clinic's Medimobile van was late. This would make seven straight months that the stupid driver didn't get to Arley's house until after five. Six months ago, Arley complained to the director of the clinic, asking how he was expected to stay alive if nobody gave a damn about getting his medicine to him when they were supposed to. The quack gave him the brush-off. Ain't nobody cares about nobody in this world, he told himself as he slammed down the phone.

Ever since, Arley took to watching from his front porch for the Free Clinic van. His house, far enough from town to avoid nosy neighbors, gave him a perfect view of the intersection of the state highway, County Road 17, and Main Street. At exactly four-o'clock on the twentieth of each month, Arley pulled a cold six-pack from the refrigerator and plopped down in the rickety porch chair. From this vantage point, he watched for the ugly blue van as it turned off the county road and started up his hill.

As he popped open his fourth beer, Arley spotted the Medimobile. In fifteen minutes it would roar up his gravel drive. He checked his watch. Four forty-eight. Draining the beer in two swallows, Arley watched the van approach the tricky three-way intersection. Thirteen more minutes until he'd be all over that driver's ass like a whore on a million-aire. Five o'clock, as Grandpa Putch would say, means five o'clock, not two minutes after. The kid would mumble an insincere "Sorry, Mr. Putch," and hightail it away as fast as he could.

A loud noise from the county road distracted Arley. Clyde Haffner's ancient poultry truck was having problems making the curve at the base of the hill. Arley silently bet that the Medimobile would make it to the intersection before the tur-key truck and looked toward the state highway to see if there'd be a third vehicle in the race.

There was. A bright red laboratory truck from the univer-sity tooled down the highway. Smart-ass rich kids out joy-riding and wasting taxpayer money, Arley figured. The speed-ing truck was Arley's bet to reach the intersection first, fol-lowed by the Medimobile, with Clyde Haffncr and the tur-keys bringing up the rear. He waited.

It didn't take long. The poultry truck lurched forward suddenly, propelling into the intersection. From the west, the university truck plowed into it, followed by the Medimobile hitting both vehicles. The resulting explosion sent a streak of bluish-purple flame whooshing skyward. Damn medicine's going up in smoke, Arley thought. He threw his beer can on the ground and headed inside, door slamming behind him. He knew the Free Clinic wouldn't send anyone else out until tomorrow. Those people didn't care about Arley Putch none.

Arley tramped through the house to the bathroom, pick-ing up the latest *World News Weekly* on his way. As he sat on the padded ring, the satisfying whoosh of air from the cush-ion gave him a small measure of comfort. Nothing like re-laxing on the crapper with the weekly edition of the truth to help a man feel better about life. He leaned back against the 'Beauchamp is My Co-Pilot' bumper sticker plastered on the tank and settled in for a good read.

When his legs began to cramp, Arley folded the tabloid

over the towel rack, yanked up his pants, and stomped into the kitchen. He rummaged through the refrigerator and found a pound of loosely wrapped hamburger. Sniffing at the brownish meat, he decided it was still okay even though it was a couple days past expiration. He checked the smiley-faced daisy clock above the cupboards. Six o'clock straight up. Time for Floyd Beauchamp.

He flipped on the once-white AM radio, now a coffee-spattered smoky gray. Beauchamp's program was about the only reason there were still radios in the Putch house. The show's host knew how to cut through crap and get to the heart of a matter. There was no mamby-pampy pampering of the 'underprivileged' for Beauchamp and none for Arley Putch neither. God-fearing Americans were first in Beauchamp's world.

"Good evening from 540AM, the all-news voice of the Valley," the announcer said. "We'll join the Floyd Beauchamp program in progress momentarily, but first this breaking news bulletin."

What the hell? Arley didn't tune in this liberal clap-trap station to hear the bleeding heart news. Where was Beauchamp?

"An accident today at the intersection of State Highway 214, Valley County Highway 17, and Main Street in Peach Hollow took the lives of four people in a three vehicle pileup. Witnesses are asked to contact the Sheriff's Tip Line at—"

He twisted the radio knob to off. Fat chance he'd call, Arley thought as he scooped a spoonful of lard into a mostly clean frying pan. Being a witness nowadays meant having some scumbag loving defense attorney tear into your past and twist normal patriotic activities into Communistic subversive behavior. Arley's cousin Vern over in Baskas County was hauled in to testify at an accident case and ended up being arrested for having unregistered guns in his trailer. No one was going to do something like that to Arley Putch. He knew his rights said he could keep his mouth shut if he wanted to.

With hamburger sizzling in the melted lard and a fresh beer on the counter, Arley flipped the radio back on. The announcer was still yammering about the accident. "The university laboratory truck was carrying a shipment of experimental bio-radioactive—"

Off with the radio again. He would catch the replay of Beauchamp later, when it wouldn't be interrupted by reporters trying to make Arley feel sorry that overpaid professors lost a precious, useless experiment. "Let 'em start over," he told the empty kitchen. "Maybe if they worked for a livin' the accident wouldn'ta happened anyhow."

Arley shoved the hamburger around the pan. "C'mon, cook already. I'm starvin'.." He downed half a can of beer and flipped the meat again. "Close enough."

He grabbed a can of Aunt Penelope's Homemade Imitation Beef Gravy from the rickety cabinet, punching a hole in the can top with a screwdriver. "Screwed you, Aunt Penelope," he laughed.

Arley dumped the contents of the can into the pan, taking culinary satisfaction in the blend of melted lard, hamburger fat and imitation beef gravy. He stirred the concoction until the goo surrounding the meat was the consistency he always aimed for—somewhere between kindergarten paste and snot. "Perfect," he pronounced, plunking his meal onto a chipped supper plate.

He dropped onto the faded blue sofa, arranging himself to avoid the spring that stabbed him in the ass if he wasn't paying attention. He balanced his supper in his lap, holding the remote control in one hand and a fresh beer in the other. "Hellfire and damnation!" he spat. "Forgot a fork." He placed his sweaty beer can on the battered end table, neatly lining it up with the crusted ring from cans past, and started to stand. "Screw it," he muttered, pulling yesterday's fork from between the couch cushions.

A punch of the remote control turned the television on

with an audible click. "And now a special report from Newscenter Thirty-Seven," the newscaster chirped.

"Pretty boy queer," Arley muttered.

"Tonight's big story…an accident on Highway 17 near Peach Hollow—"

Arley flipped the television to the all-sports channel. "I saw the accident," he told the TV. "I don't need to hear 'bout it, too."

Within fifteen minutes of sloshing the last forkful of his meat recipe into his mouth, Arley was snoring, dish still balanced on his torn T-shirt clad belly. His dozing was interrupted by an alarm sound coming from his television. He peered at the set through sleep-filled eyes.

"The accident on Highway 17 has claimed more—"

He clicked the television off. How could they interrupt sports for news? He'd have to call that damn cable company tomorrow and give them a piece of his mind. Not that nobody there cared if a disabled man got his entertainment or not.

Arley looked at the sunburst clock above the television. Almost eleven-thirty. Time for the replay of the Beauchamp show. He'd climb into bed, turn on the bedside radio, and give a listen. Arley stood, the forgotten supper dish falling face down on the shag rug. "Damnation!" He shoved the dinner plate under the couch, telling himself he'd pick it up tomorrow.

In his bedroom, Arley stripped to his boxers, glad to be free of his pants. Damn things shrunk in the wash again since the laundromat didn't know how to control their water temperature. Ruined all his clothes going there. He complained, but it didn't do no good. Nobody gave a damn about Arley Putch anyway.

Arley climbed under his torn army blanket. Tonight was the second part of Beauchamp's discussion of illegal aliens working at fast food restaurants and Arley didn't want to miss it. It was so bad down to the Burger Barn that he couldn't step foot inside without stepping on one of the little greaseballs. He turned on the radio.

"The fallout from that accident on Highway 17 outside of Peach Hollow continues to—"

Arley threw the radio across the room, watching it shatter on the yellow wall. "Damn piece of Jap crap," he declared, angrily turning the bedside light off. The station interrupted Floyd Beauchamp for the second time in one day! They'd get a phone call in the morning, not that they'd care.

He drifted off quickly, dreaming of the country the way it would be if he and Floyd Beauchamp ran things. Fierce pounding at the door woke him up just as President Putch signed the order to send all the gays and liberals to Canada. "Putch! Putch! It's Sheriff Grogan! Open up!"

What was that idiot yelling about in the middle of the night? The sheriff hadn't been out since somebody said Arley was hunting too close to the highway. If he didn't leave soon, Arley'd blast him away.

"Putch! Open up! It's about the accident!"

A man couldn't even sleep in his own house in the middle of the night anymore without Communists banging on his damn door. He wasn't listening to anything about that accident no more. Everything was dark outside, so there wasn't any fire and there wasn't no need to rustle himself out of bed in the middle of the night to talk to the law. The sheriff could go—

He heard the door of the police cruiser open and close. Good, Arley thought, laughing as the sheriff's car squealed away into the night. Now maybe he could get some rest. "No wonder this country's so screwed up," Arley grumbled as he punched his pillow. "Disturbin' a man over an accident that he ain't even part of. I ain't never gonna get back to sleep. Not that nobody gives a damn anyways."

Arley woke a little before noon. He lifted himself from the bed, yawning and rubbing his belly. Damn fool sheriff, he thought. Screwed up a perfectly good snooze.

He padded to the bathroom, dropped his boxers and sat on the toilet. "Goodbye, Aunt Penelope." His laugh echoed around the small room, the answering silence reminding him that it was time for the Wayne Lester show. Lester wasn't near as good an American as Beauchamp, but his show was perfect to crap by. He grumbled as he leaned over and twisted the knob on the transistor radio tied to the toilet paper dispenser.

"The mysterious substance that has covered a large portion of the valley as a result of yesterday's three vehicle accident is still spreading. Professor Egbert Waverman from the university research laboratory refused to speculate on the composition of the brown, tar-like substance, but has confirmed that it is apparently still feeding on every living organism and inanimate object in its path. County Sheriff Ficus Grogan tells All News 540 AM that the valley was evacuated before the growth spread and that all residents are believed safe."

Arley looked at the bathroom window. Brown glop covered it, guppy-mouthed suckers squiggling on the glass. "They coulda told a guy what was goin' on," he said as the window frame cracked and started to bow. "Nobody cares about Arley Putch. Nobody at all."

Michael Giorgio is an advertising accountant, writer, and radio dramatist living in Waukesha, Wisconsin with his beautiful writer wife, Kathie, daughter Olivia, stepchildren Christopher, Andy, and Katie, one dog, two cats, one bird, one guinea pig, and whoever else wanders in. (http://hometown.aol.com/mgiorgio1/)

CAUGHT WITH HIS PANTS DOWN

Alice heard movement in her bathroom the moment she entered her apartment. She'd thought she'd seen Harry's car parked on the street, so she'd entered with stealth.

He'd come to hurt her. She knew that much, but nothing else.

Down the hallway, she saw that the bathroom door was open, but Alice didn't advance far enough to see in. She crept into her bedroom, careful to step over the creaky spot in the floor. She eased open her vanity's slim drawer, and found one of her makeup bags empty. Her gun wasn't where she'd left it. *How the hell did he know where to find it?*

She'd risked entering the apartment because she thought the gun gave her the upper hand, but now . . .

Stupid, stupid, stupid, she thought. Why hadn't she called the police instead of confronting Harry alone? She knew why — she just didn't want to admit it to herself. A part of her wanted an excuse to shoot Harry. An excuse to *kill* Harry in self-defense. Her hand went involuntarily to the deep scar that ran from her left ear to her chin.

The bathroom cupboard closed with a thump. Alice jumped. She didn't know what he was looking for, but then she figured he was just snooping to kill time while he waited for her. Waited to finish what he'd started a year ago. She knew she should get out of the apartment before he left the bathroom. But she didn't move, paralyzed by fear, her back to the bedroom door. What if he'd already left the bathroom?

Maybe he's standing behind me.

Watching. Waiting.

Then she heard something that sounded like a zipper. The next sounds disgusted and delighted her.

Now's my chance, she thought. Sneak out while he's otherwise occupied. Alice left the bedroom, but an uncontrollable urge led her down the hall to the bathroom instead of out the front door. She had to know for sure that it was him.

The splashes were loud and continuous, so she screwed up her courage and peeked her head through the bathroom doorway. Despite her expectations, she hardly believed her eyes, and had to stifle a gasp. A broad-shouldered man with light brown hair, wearing jeans and a jean jacket, stood in front of the toilet with his back to Alice. She didn't need to see the front of his face to know it was definitely Harry.

To Alice's left, she saw her gun on the counter next to the sink. She didn't stop to think. She just grabbed it.

Her swift movement reflected in the mirror and caught Harry's attention. He looked over his shoulder in surprise. Then he smirked. "So," he said, motioning downward diagonally with his eyes, "you like the show?"

He continued to relieve himself. He must've had a dozen beers before coming over, Alice thought. She pointed the gun at him, and just stood there. Shaking. She didn't know what to do — she was so scared and *angry*!

"If you plan to use that gun," Harry said, "you'd better hurry up. 'Cuz when I'm through with this *piss*-tol, I'm going to yank that one out of your hands."

"I'm going to call the cops," Alice said. "They'll send you back to jail. This time for good."

"Yeah, right. Look, honey, that's your gun. So they can't

charge me with possession. And I ain't threatened you with it. So what're they gonna do? Charge me with pissing in my ex-girlfriend's apartment?" He snickered. "I don't even think they'll charge me with trespassing since this was a real emergency."

Infuriated and distracted by the sound of Harry's tenth beer exiting his body, Alice couldn't think of an adequate response. "They can charge you with being drunk and disorderly," Alice said, knowing how lame the threat sounded.

"Just let me go," he said. "Don't worry I won't touch you. I promise." He smiled insincerely. "Just like I *promised* before that I wouldn't be satisfied until you're as ugly as you made me feel when you dumped me. I keep my promises. I'll get you when you least expect it. . . ."

Fear and rage intermingled to cloud Alice's judgment. She wanted Harry out of her life, *now*. She had to scare him away.

Now.

The gun fired. The bullet ripped through the rear pocket of Harry's jeans.

It felt good to hurt him, to give him a humiliating wound. It felt good for a split second. Then it felt very, very bad.

When the bullet smashed into Harry's buttock, he jerked forward. His shin hit the toilet bowl, which caused him to fall backwards to the side. Alice watched in horror as his head cracked open upon impact with the ceramic bathtub.

"Omigod, I killed him!" Alice shrieked, and dropped the gun. No sooner were the words out of her mouth, when she pictured herself being tried for murder and one of her neighbors testifying that they'd heard the gunshot then her confession.

"It was self-defense!" she shouted to the potential witnesses. "He would've made good on his promise. . . ."

They won't believe me, she thought.

She had to get out of there. Run away. She could never come back.

Alice hastily opened the cupboard to grab a few essentials. Harry groaned, and she spun around with her face cream in hand.

He's not dead!

Harry groped for the gun. His fingers closed on the grip, and Alice screamed. She dropped the cream and ran out of the bathroom.

The jar smashed on the tile floor with a loud bang that caused Alice's hair to stand on end. She knew the next bang would be worse.

Even as she slammed the apartment door behind her, she expected a bullet to tear through the wood, but Harry never fired the gun. Despite her hatred and fear, Alice didn't leave the building. She banged on her neighbors' doors until someone answered, then called for an ambulance. She'd felt like a murderer for a few seconds, and she never wanted to feel that way again.

"It was self-defense! Don't you believe me?"

"I have to finish taking your statement, Ms. Joppler." The policeman tapped his pen on the pad of paper on Alice's kitchen table.

"Call me Alice. Look, officer, I really had no choice. What would you have done?"

The policeman tried to keep a straight face. "I would've let him finish his, er, business. Then I would've tried talking to him."

"We did talk! About him promising to finish what he'd started. See this?" She pointed at the scar that ran from her left ear to her chin. "He did this last year. And all he got was one year! I knew the bastard would come after me the first chance he got — parole be damned."

"Oh, yes . . . I remember your case. They called Arze the copycat mangler, because he copied that psycho who slashed that model's face. The old 'if I can't have her, nobody will' thing."

"Yeah, except I was never a beautiful model."

"Well, if you ask me, he failed, because you're still a very attractive woman." Alice blushed, and the policeman hurriedly changed the subject. "Ahem, so let me make sure I have this straight. He threatened you, you shot him. You dropped the gun, he reached for the gun, you threw a jar at him."

"Yes, that's pretty much what happened. Except I dropped the jar out of fear. I didn't *throw it* at him."

"What was in that jar, Alice?"

"Vitamin E cream. It's supposed to help get rid of scars."

The policeman frowned. "That's all?"

"Yeah — what's the big deal?" Alice asked.

"Didn't you see what it did to his neck?"

"No, I ran out of there before he could shoot me."

"Well—" The policeman's mobile phone rang. "Excuse me." He stood and walked out of earshot. As he conversed, his face went through a range of emotions, from professional interest, to shock, to horror.

Alice fidgeted in her seat. What was going on? What did Harry tell the police in the ambulance? Were they going to arrest her?

The policeman finished his call and then spoke with two other officers at the scene. As he walked back to the table, the other two split up and went to Alice's bedroom and bathroom.

"There's no easy way to put this," the policeman said once seated. "Harry Arze is dead."

Alice gasped. "I killed him," she whispered, lowering her head.

"No, you didn't"

Her head snapped back up. "What? How'd he die?"

"Acid ate through his neck to his windpipe, and he suffocated en route to the hospital."

Alice didn't hide her confusion.

"The officers with him were confused too, but then they noticed that Arze had some makeup on his fingers. That seemed odd, so they checked his pockets. They found empty containers of prussic acid, glycolic acid, and sulfuric acid. We're certain that he put one of those acids into your skin cream, and the others somewhere else. He evidently wanted to make sure that he *destroyed* your face this time. We're confiscating all of your cosmetics, and just to be safe, all liquids from this apartment. We'll return everything that our labs deem safe."

Alice shuddered.

"Are you alright?"

Alice nodded as she thought about what the officer had just told her.

"Given the circumstances, I'm going to report the shooting as self-defense. Just one thing I don't understand — why'd you pick up the cream in the first place?"

Alice shuddered again. If she'd actually packed and ran away, she would've helped Harry keep his promise. She forced herself to smile at the policeman. "Well, you see, I ummm . . ."

The policeman smiled, and she thought she saw a twinkle in his eyes. "Oh, that's right. I have here in my notes that you threw it at him when he picked up the gun. Well, Ms. Joppler, you are one lucky lady."

Alice smiled gratefully. She sure was one lucky lady — a lucky lady who got to save face.

Nick Andreychuk is a Derringer Award-winning author. His stories can be found in Crimestalker Casebook, DOWN THESE DARK STREETS, FEDORA I & III, Futures Mysterious Anthology Magazine, HARD-BROILED, MURDER BY SIX, and Shred of Evidence, among many others. Nick's work can also be found in BULLET POINTS, an anthology of short-short crime fiction that he co-edited.

NEVER TRUST A POISON DART FROG

It was Friday when Ted finally realized he had to do something about Irene. After forty-two years of marriage, he had had enough.

He sat down in his worn, comfortable easy chair after a hard week at the accounting firm, thoughts of retirement in two years tumbling through his mind. He sighed, ready to lose himself in a spy novel. Ready to relax.

Then Irene stomped up and crossed her arms over her small, wilted breasts.

"Get out of that chair."

Ted looked over the top of his reading glasses at the curled lip now six inches from his face. He flinched.

"What now?"

"You know what now. Take the dog for a walk."

"I'm tired. I'll do it later."

"Now. The dog has waited all day for you to take it out."

"You walk the dog."

"Are you trying to kill me? You know the doctor says I need rest for my heart condition."

It was right then that the idea struck Ted. Divorce was out of the question; he'd lose the house and most of his savings. But if she were to die, he would have the peace and quiet he sought. He licked his lips in anticipation. He would find a final solution.

Ted slowly rose to his feet.

"Now that you're up, take out the garbage and change the light bulb in the hall. You never notice when lights are burned out. I can't believe how oblivious you are to what goes on around here."

"Yes, dear."

"Thelma's husband does all the gardening and home repair without her having to say anything. You don't do anything. I have to constantly remind you. What's wrong with you? Are you listening to me?"

What's wrong with me is I'm stuck with you, Ted thought. What he said was, "Yes, dear."

On Saturday after receiving a tongue-lashing for leaving his orange juice glass in the sink rather than washing it, Ted drove to the library.

He located a book on lethal poisons, found a quiet table in a remote stack, and began reading. There were so many choices, but all seemed to have some drawback.

After an hour his back began to ache.

After two hours he was ready to give up when one caught his eye. The poison of the Golden Poison Dart Frog, *Phyllobates terribilis* from the rain forests of Colombia, South America. He read that the batrachotoxin on the skin of this two-inch long, golden yellow frog produced heart failure in humans. Local tribes used the poison on blowgun darts to kill prey instantly. The poison could be transmitted even through unbroken skin. One frog had enough poison to kill a hundred humans.

Wow, Ted thought. Powerful stuff. If Irene were to die of heart failure, it would be just what her doctor expected and what she constantly told all her friends was about to happen. All he needed was a Golden Poison Dart Frog.

He returned the book and skulked over to one of the public access Internet computers. He jerked his head around to make sure no one was watching him, then sat down. After many fruitless searches, he found a reference that made his heart beat faster. There was a company fifty miles away that sold exotic animals. Their inventory included rare frogs. They were even open until six P.M. on Saturdays.

Ted wrote down the address, logged off the computer and dashed out to his car.

Later that afternoon he hummed "Tonight" from *West Side Story* as he placed the aerated box on his workbench in the garage. Only fifty dollars to purchase his freedom, using cash he had hidden in a coffee can in the garage.

Entering the house, he was assailed by Irene.

"It's about time you got home. Where have you been? I've got this table to move. You know I can't do it myself. You'll be the death of me yet."

"Yes, dear," Ted said with a broad smile.

Ted had decided just how to do it. While Irene was taking her late afternoon nap, he retrieved the wash cloth from the bathroom sink, a knife from the kitchen, and a pair of rubber gloves from the pantry cupboard.

He slipped on the gloves and went to the garage. He opened the box and two large eyes stared up at him.

Sorry, Buddy, Ted thought, but you've got to give your skin for an important cause.

He returned the wash cloth, now saturated in the liquid from the frog's skin, to the bathroom sink. Every night before going to bed, Irene scrubbed her face almost raw with this wash cloth. Tonight it would solve his problem.

After thoroughly washing the knife, he sealed the frog remains and gloves in a plastic bag. Whistling "Happy Days are Here Again," he took the dog for a walk and deposited the plastic bag in a dumpster three blocks away. Then he returned home to take a shower.

"What's all the noise," Irene cried, having awakened from

her nap.

"Just going to take a shower."

"Don't use all the hot water."

The stream surged off his head and sprayed around the shower stall. He was so preoccupied with his thoughts of quiet time by himself that when he stepped out of the tub he forgot to duck his head.

He even heard the loud "crack" as his head bashed the sliding rail of the shower.

"What's that?" Irene shouted from the bedroom. She pulled the bathroom door open.

Ted stood dazed, half in and half out of the tub with blood spilling from his forehead.

"What stupid thing have you done now?" Irene sputtered.

She grabbed the washcloth from the sink and thrust it against Ted's forehead to stem the flow of blood.

"No!" Ted bellowed. He grabbed his chest and pitched forward onto the bathroom floor.

The paramedics removed Ted's body from the bathroom to the shrill sound of Irene's complaint that her stupid husband didn't have the dignity to die of heart failure with his clothes on.

A week later she started cleaning out the garage and discovered the box on the workbench. Inside was a folded sheet. She removed the tape, opened the single page and read: "You will enjoy your Golden Poison Dart Frog for as many as four years with the proper vivarium, fresh water, and diet of crickets, ants, and termites. Be assured that this is a safe pet because Golden Poison Dart Frogs kept and bred in captivity are not poisonous."

Mike Befeler turned his attention to fiction writing after a career in high technology marketing. He is working on a collection of short stories and a three book mystery series. He holds a Master's degree from UCLA and a Bachelor's degree from Stanford.

WASH AWAY MY SIN

Manny entered his remodeled bathroom. His wife's eyes were closed and billowing bubbles enveloped her.

Four pillars, with cascading netting, stood as centurions to the raised marbled platform where the tub rested. The tub was surrounded with black and gold marbled counters with mahogany drawers reflected in gold-framed mirrors.

Stephanie heard him moving. "Hmm, this is *wonderful*! Long wait, but you got it done in time."

Manny grunted.

"My sisters will arrive at three this afternoon. They are going to be so envious."

Manny thought she elongated the word "so" with the delight of someone who loves to impress others. Her *sisters* weren't blood relatives but former sorority sisters. Stephanie had invited them for their annual reunion gab fest. For weeks, she had nagged him to remodel the bathroom.

As a contractor, this was his best work. He installed extras only he knew about. He studied his muscular body in his reflection. Not bad. Stephanie didn't know it, but he was eager for her pals to arrive. Hot chicks, all of them! He licked his lips in anticipation. He'd seen their photos in all the yearbooks his wife had been shoving under his nose for months.

"I can't wait to see Roni," Stephanie prattled on. "We suffered many hangovers together in our younger days." Her tone stiffened as she asked, "You're going to change, right?"

To Manny, it sounded more like a command than a question. "What would you like me to wear?" he asked.

"I've already laid your ensemble out on the bed."

Ensemble. Can't she just say clothes? "Okay."

As he turned to leave, Stephanie warned him, "And, it's hands off Manny! None of your tricks! They're off limits."

Manny nodded silently and ducked out. Silence, he'd discovered, brought less trouble than trying to defend himself. He paused a moment outside the door. If she only knew, a smile crawled across his lips as he shut the door.

He made his way down to the basement since his wife would be busy for the next hour. One last check. He'd finished the majority of the basement into a bar and party room. He pushed an obscure door, which blended in illusion to the paneled walls. It led to his workshop and the corral for anything that he wanted in the house that didn't meet Stephanie's definition of exquisite decorating. Most of his "things," save his clothes, had been relegated to this room. He'd rescued his favorite battered easy chair from the trash after Stephanie hired someone to set it at the curb.

Manny went to his corner workbench, purposely kept dirty and cluttered. Stephanie wouldn't even step into this room and that was just the way Manny liked it. He checked the new wiring and the connections at the junction box. He couldn't wait.

At three o'clock Stephanie's gaggle began to arrive. Spiffed, shined, and smiling, Manny stood at Stephanie's side to greet her guests. She sent him to make drinks. He studied each woman as he circulated. For the most part, the women were unseeing, except for Roni who willed with her eyes and pressed her knee against his leg. The others paid him no attention, so intent on their gossiping, that he would exchange empty glasses for a full drink, without them realizing. It gave him the opportunity to study their physiques and pick those he was most interested in. Like an undercover movie producer, he was searching for his next star. Or stars. He relished the thought.

Stephanie ushered her girlfriends on the anticipated house tour. She complimented Manny freely, pointing out all the remodeling and building he'd done. She saved the bathroom until last. "You'll all have to share this."

Stephanie glowed among the comments from her sorority sisters. *How beautiful! This is exquisite! I feel like I'm in a castle.* Manny saw it all, but he wasn't with them. He settled back contentedly in his tattered chair with pretzels and a beer. He stared hungrily at the remote picture dancing across the monitor's screen. He flipped on the video recorder to make sure everything was working properly. When not in use, he hid the remote monitor and recorder underneath a box with the bottom cut out. It was a box on which Stephanie had printed in big block letters "Dirty and Greasy Things." In it she had collected tools and parts that he left on the kitchen counter when they first moved in. It was a perfect hiding place. She'd never look in the box and discover his set up.

He had carefully placed hidden cameras in his new bathroom, so tiny as not to be noticeable. There wasn't a bit he couldn't see. The women would be going out for a females-only dinner soon ... and getting ready. *Let the show begin!* His body trembled with excitement as he watched each woman enter. Their lingerie, the way they walked, the way they leaned over to peer in the mirror to apply mascara, the curves of their hips and breasts in all different sizes. Sarah had the longest hair. Roni had the laciest lingerie; Cybil the skimpiest. Sylvia had the biggest, well-rounded hips and booty. Terry was too thin but had cute breasts. He loved it all! This was heaven!

Manny checked the locked cabinet labeled "Oil and Car

Parts." On one side, his fingers caressed his past video re-
cordings. New tapes, still in their shrink wrap glittered at
him on the other side. He had stocked up on his supply in
anticipation of this weekend. This wouldn't be the first time
he recorded Roni. Not that she knew. Roni and he dated
briefly in college, but she dumped him for another jock on
the football team. He'd met Stephanie through Roni, since
they were roommates. He licked his lips, as he relished the
ability to compare Roni ten years ago with how she looked
now. She still looked good with her clothes on!

Later that night, the girls returned, giddy with too much
alcohol. Manny had moved his car, so Stephanie would assume he was at his favorite local bar. Instead, he relaxed
comfortably in his chair, eyes riveted to the flickering monitor for his evening entertainment. *Beautiful.* He didn't care
what they did, whether they were chunky or skinny. He loved
watching. His heart raced a bit faster as each woman entered
and left the bathroom. For once, he could be thankful for
Stephanie's constant nagging.

Manny sat up when Roni entered the luxurious bathroom.
She didn't use any of the facilities. Roni moved surrepti-
tiously, quietly, as if she was afraid of being watched, or heard.
She set down a big tote bag she carried and began opening all
of the drawers, one by one. Manny laughed. He'd always
wondered how many of their guests snooped when they knew
they wouldn't be caught. Now he'd know, exactly who did.

Manny saw her extract Stephanie's bottle of vitamin capsules from a drawer and study the bottle. Then she dropped it
into her bag. She's taking a bottle of vitamins? He recalled
Stephanie telling Roni about them when Roni asked for her
secret to looking vibrant. Their competition never ended.
Manny was further puzzled when she reached in her purse
and withdrew the bottle of vitamins. He watched as Roni then
grabbed a tissue and wiped the bottle and every drawer handle
she touched and left the bathroom. *A guilty conscience?*

He checked his watch. Time to make an appearance. He

left by the back door and walked around the block where he retrieved his car to "return" home. The house had quieted and he climbed the stairs and went straight to the bathroom. Out of curiosity, he went directly to his wife's pill drawer and pulled out the bottle of vitamins. He opened it and poured the half empty contents into his hand. Nothing looked wrong with the capsules. He put them back in the bottle and tossed it back into the drawer. Stephanie staggered in the bathroom, just as he was leaving. "We had such a good time," she said, slurring her words. He caught her as she teetered precariously. "Be a dear, Manny, and turn out the downstairs lights for me. I've got a headache. Stephanie had left most of the lights on, probably to show off the house when they returned. Fifteen minutes later, he walked into a darkened bedroom, a familiar practice. Quietly, he undressed. She didn't even move when he crawled into bed. He fell asleep dreaming happily about all the viewing opportunities he'd have tomorrow.

The next morning, Manny was surprised to see Stephanie still in bed. He heard the others stirring in the house and decided to get up to fix them breakfast. He glanced at his wife again, who was sleeping on her side, with her back to him. Something seemed odd, out-of-place. He nudged her. She felt different. He walked around to her side of the bed and peered closely. A deep purple stain seemed to have pooled on the bottom side of her face. He shook her and called her name, then withdrew his hand as if his fingers had been burned. Stephanie was dead. His heart jolted with the realization. He picked up the phone and called 9-1-1.

A deafening quiet had settled over the house in the weeks since Stephanie's death. Her sorority sisters had been devastated. Roni organized them to help him with all the funeral arrangements. Now they were gone and Manny roamed aimlessly from room to room in his house. Beautiful, but not very clean nor organized now. Each room had dirty dishes, half eaten sandwiches, or soiled clothes strewn about. Manny didn't even notice.

The doorbell rang, and he trudged to the door. The simplest acts seemed to require inordinate amounts of effort. Nothing really mattered, he thought. Even seeing a salesman would be a welcome relief from his grief. When he opened the door, he was surprised to find Detective Hawkins standing on the porch with his partner, Pete Lowrey. They flashed their badges, which was unnecessary, since they had come when he placed the emergency call, the morning he'd discovered Stephanie.

"May we come in?" Hawkins asked. "We need to talk to you."

Manny nodded and opened the door wider to let them pass. He ushered them into the living room and swept newspapers off the sofa and tossed a shirt and jacket on the floor.

"The toxicology reports came back," Hawkins stated. "Your wife didn't die of natural causes, as we first thought."

"She didn't?" Manny's mind fogged.

"The report indicates that she was poisoned," Hawkins stated.

Manny stared blankly at Hawkins who seemed to be studying him intently. "Poisoned?" It seemed like a foreign word as he repeated it.

"We also tested several of the objects we removed that day. You told us that your wife often took vitamins."

"Yes, she's a health food nut and she'd take them to redeem herself after drinking at parties."

"We took her bottle that night to test the contents and for fingerprints." Hawkins nodded to Lowrey, who moved closer to Manny. "We found your wife's....and we found yours."

"So?"

"The capsules didn't contain vitamin powder. They contained a potent sedative. A deadly sedative when combined with alcohol. More importantly, your fingerprints are the only ones found on the capsules in the bottle. Manny Tate, we're placing you under arrest for the murder of your wife, Stephanie." To his partner he said, "Read him his rights."

Detective Lowrey pulled his wrists behind Manny's back and slapped handcuffs on him, while reciting the Miranda.

Details of that night, of watching the girls, of Roni, taking then not taking the vitamin bottle, flooded back to him. *I'm keeping my mouth shut. I'm going to need help to get out of this one.* He knew now who killed his wife. But how could he tell without revealing his own unorthodox hobby? "I want my lawyer."

"You can call from the station," Detective Hawkins explained to him, "after you've been processed."

Later, Manny sat in a small, sparsely furnished room and whispered to his attorney. *Thank goodness for attorney/client privilege. If word got out what he'd been doing, his construction business would dry up quicker than a raisin.* His attorney, using his legal beagle language, persuaded the district attorney to release him. Once they saw the video tape, they had no reason to hold him. Lucky for him, they couldn't arrest him for videotaping in the first place. His lawyer explained that, through a loophole in the state's law, surveillance of one's home is permitted and because he never distributed the images, nor ever recorded a minor, they couldn't touch him. Still, Manny heard the disgust in the officer's voice when he was released. His attorney stringently urged him to find a new hobby.

In cooperation with the law enforcement agencies in her state, Roni was arrested the next day. Confronted with the overwhelming evidence, she confessed. The district attorney charged her with premeditated murder. The judge remanded her to life imprisonment with possible parole.

After the brief sentencing hearing, Manny returned home. The cute real estate agent was waiting for him. He signed the sales agreement and then retrieved his toolbox from his truck to help her erect the "For Sale" sign in his front yard. He'd move to a new place and build himself a grand house. He could afford it, especially with the proceeds from Stephanie's life insurance policy. After all, no one would expect a grieving widower to stay in the house where his wife died.

He waved good-bye to the real estate agent and carried his toolbox inside. The agent was bringing someone to see the house this evening. She had suggested that he light a fire in the fireplace. He opened his toolbox and removed the tray, then the bulky tools to reach the false bottom. He lifted it and extracted the letter he'd received from Roni a month before the sorority reunion. She had divorced earlier in the year and regretted the years lost without Manny. She wanted him back. While she was awaiting her sentencing, he visited her in prison. Roni was jealous of Stephanie and what she thought was her perfect marriage. She was envious of the new house and bathroom. She thought it all should be hers. He tossed the letter into the flames.

Manny carried his toolbox up to the bathroom and removed the cameras and their wiring to the video recorder. He also opened a panel beneath the tub and removed the extra wires he'd installed. Stephanie no longer needed to have an "accident" by electrocution in her tub. Manny went down to his workroom and removed the switch he never needed to use.

How was he to know that Roni had the same idea to get rid of Stephanie? Roni got what she deserved too. She never should have dumped him.

Peggy Jaegly is a freelance writer living in Hillsborough, New Jersey. She combines her musical and storytelling talents as a professional certified bedside harpist serving hospitals and nursing homes throughout New Jersey and the Greater Baltimore Area.

THE BIG LEAGUE

The detective looked past the patrol officer's shoulder into the restroom. "Who discovered the body?"

"A little league team returning from an away game. Each of the players claims he saw the legs sticking out of the stall first. They're waiting for you on the bus."

"Did you tell them not to talk about the incident?"

"Sir?"

"Right. Stupid question. I have a boy that age of my own. What about the coach? I assume he's on the bus too."

The officer shook his head and motioned with his thumb towards the bathroom. "That's him in the second stall."

"The coach is the victim?"

"They all identified him, even with the blood covering his face."

"Blood?"

"Looks like a blunt instrument to the forehead. The way it appears to me, someone opened the stall door and popped him one while he was sitting on the toilet."

"Okay. Good work officer."

"Thanks."

The detective entered the bathroom and stopped just inside, examining the perimeter first. There were three windows set high, closed and covered with unbroken wire mesh.

Unfortunately, he didn't see any evidence of surveillance cameras which may have made his life a lot easier.

A little league team's worth of dirty footprints covered the floor.

The detective slipped back out into the hall. "Were there any other adults, chaperones?"

The uniformed officer shook his head. "Only the coach who doubled as driver."

"Gotcha."

Back in the bathroom, the detective stared at the legs visible from under the second stall.

"So the coach stops the bus, tells the boys to wait, and goes into the bathroom first to make sure it's safe: no perverts, no drug dealers, no hookers. After checking the place, he decides to relieve himself, overhears something he shouldn't, and signals his presence by making a sound. The dealer or whatever whacks him and flees. The boys, tired of sitting on the bus, come in and discover the body."

The detective walked over to the stall and pushed open the door.

It looked like a blunt instrument all right.

"Why didn't the dealer or whoever make certain the bathroom was empty before conducting business? Why kill the coach and chance leaving forensic evidence when he probably couldn't identify the people involved?"

The detective crouched to check if the coach's wallet was missing. It wasn't. Money and charge cards, right where they belonged.

"Business cards. Our coach sells insurance, not exactly a career which incites murder."

The detective stood.

"So maybe it was a thrill kill. Someone waits outside for his victim to go into the bathroom, clubs him, and then takes off. But wouldn't he have seen the bus loaded with kids? Too much chance of a witness."

He took a deep breath.

"There's no evidence that he banged his head on the toilet paper dispenser, no reason to believe his death was an accident. Suicide is out of the question."

The detective thought about the boys sitting out on the bus.

He stepped back into the hall. "The away game. Did they win or lose?"

"I think they lost."

"I was afraid you'd say that."

———————

Stephen D. Rogers has published over 250 stories and poems that have been selected to appear in more than a hundred publications. When not setting down words, he is busy keeping www.stephendrogers.com safe for visitors.

Bev Vincent

WHAT DAVID WAS DOING WHEN THE LIGHTS WENT OUT

The Blackout of 2003 they were calling it, and it was David Emerson's fault. Of all the things he expected might happen, this wasn't one of them.

Maybe a prolonged sizzling when he dropped the hair dryer into the bathtub next to his wife. The smell of burning wire or flesh. Perhaps some of those dancing blue lines they showed in movies when someone was electrocuted. Then a circuit breaker would trip.

Instead, there'd only been a barely perceptible pop. Jen had stiffened briefly, splashing a little water over the bathtub's edge onto the mat and then the lights went out. When they hadn't come back on a few minutes later, he looked out the window and realized that the outage extended beyond their apartment.

After searching through boxes and drawers in their storage room – once a nursery and, later, Billy's bedroom–he found an old portable radio. He used the batteries from Jen's portable CD player, the one she took with her to the gym to work out on the treadmill (and why couldn't he go to the gym more, after all they were paying good money every month, and she was the only one using it, and did he think those love handles were just going to go away on their own?), and found a news station that told him the magnitude of the outage.

Fifty million people without electricity across northeastern United States because he'd had enough of Jen's incessant haranguing.

He'd planned on sneaking out of their thirty-eighth floor apartment and down the fire stairs after the deed was done. In the lobby he'd make a show of arriving home from the cinema–he'd purchased a ticket for the late afternoon showing of a movie he'd watched the previous day–talk to the manager for a few minutes to establish his alibi, take the elevator up to their apartment and discover–*quelle horreur*–his dead wife.

He'd tell everyone how many times he had warned her it wasn't safe to keep a hair dryer plugged in so close to the bathtub. Playing the part of the grieving husband wouldn't be all that hard for he was sincerely sorry things had reached the point where murder was the only way out of their relationship.

He hadn't counted on a short circuit taking out the electricity. Not only in the apartment or the building, not only on their block or even in part of Manhattan. The whole freakin' northeast and midwest. And part of Canada, too.

The stairwell was full of people, so he couldn't risk leaving without running into someone who could place him in the building when he was supposed to be watching a movie. Not having been at the theater, he didn't know during what scene in the movie the power had gone out.

Officials didn't know the power disruption's cause yet. A fire at a power plant in upstate New York, perhaps, or a lightning strike in Ontario. David knew differently. Could they trace the power surge to his block, to their building, to this very apartment?

He thought they might be able to.

From their apartment window he watched the chaos below. People streamed into the streets to find out what had happened, adding to the confusion at intersections where the traffic signals had gone dark. If he hadn't been on vacation this week he'd be part of that group, milling about idly on the streets, wondering how he was going to get home.

In the bathroom, his wife's body was slowly cooling off in lavender-scented bath water.

What should he do? He hated having to come up with something on the spur of the moment. Planning things out in detail well in advance, that was how he preferred to operate.

Maybe he *could* go downstairs with the others and trust that amid the pandemonium no one would notice him. Who would remember him when the city was in crisis? Was it worth the risk? He knew from TV that all it took for murderers to get caught was one oversight. Something so trivial it went unmarked at the time.

Better he should stay in the apartment.

Under normal circumstances–if he hadn't known his wife was already dead–he would have checked on Jen immediately when the power went out. That David, the one who hadn't just murdered his wife, would find her unresponsive. His hand would eventually come upon the power cord and he would pull the hair dryer, dripping, from the tub and understand what had happened.

Then what? Call for help. In his mind he'd rehearsed the 911 call, how he'd react when he "got back from the movies" and found Jen dead in the tub. He no longer trusted his acting skills to pull it off. If he called 911 now, emergency crews would be backed up helping free people stuck in elevators and stalled subway trains. But how would it look if he didn't call?

Then there was the matter of the alibi. Husbands were the prime suspects when wives were found dead under suspicious circumstances. He considered several possibilities.

Pretend to be stuck in an elevator? No, they might send someone and find out he wasn't there. Busted.

Call the apartment from his cell phone and leave a mes-

sage, pretending he had no way to get home because the sub-
ways were down, the streets were congested with people and
the taxis weren't stopping for anyone? That had possibilities, but when he turned on his cell phone the screen said NO
SERVICE. No service, no alibi.

In the near-darkness he wandered around the apartment
where they had lived most of their married life. They couldn't
really afford the place on his salary alone, but Jen had insisted a Lower Manhattan address would look good on his
resume and would help him get the career advancements she
had mapped out for him.

And they needed room for the two children she had
planned. A boy followed by a girl, two years apart. She had
subjected David to a series of revolting potions and brews
she'd read about on the Internet to ensure that Billy came out
first and not Brittany.

Miracle of miracles, it had worked. Billy was born right
on schedule during the third year of their marriage, but there
had never been a Brittany. It was David's fault, of course,
though every test he took–without complaint–showed that his
little guys were swimming nimbly and in sufficient quantity
to sire a football team of Emersons.

More potions, more brews. No Brittany.

Billy's cancer was his fault, too. Weak genes, according
to his wife, her sisters and their mother. David gave the others the benefit of the doubt and assumed they didn't know he
could overhear them when the subject came up, but Jen had
said this to his face after a longer-than-usual tirade, and he
had shouldered the guilt without argument. Long ago he had
discovered that disagreeing with Jennifer only led to more
heated diatribes where she talked over anything he tried to
say. Discussions like those ended as if he hadn't disputed her
statements in the first place, so he gave up.

He spoke less and less, turned a deaf ear to most of what
she said and uttered the requisite grunting acknowledgements
based on the pauses, crests, and valleys of her monologues.

He wore the clothes she laid out for him in the morning before work even when he wouldn't have selected a color combination quite so gaudy, fashion impaired though he might be. The day before business trips, he allowed her to brand him with a livid hickey, visible above his collar, to make sure any women he encountered knew he was spoken for.

When they dined out, she chose the restaurant, ordered for both of them, and ate from his plate without asking. If they left the city by car, he drove, following her precise directions. Even if he knew her instructions were wrong, he followed them and accepted the blame when she realized they were off course. He must have turned left when she had clearly told him to go right.

The only place where he could say what was on his mind was at work, and there he discovered–after reducing two secretaries to tears–that he'd lost the ability to be tactful when Jen wasn't there to rein him in. He knew his coworkers talked about him behind his back from the way they fell silent when he entered the lunchroom, but he didn't care. He had chosen this life and if it wasn't perfect, well, whose was? They had endured years of treatments, remissions, relapses, false hope, and despair with Billy. They had practically lived in the hospital for months and their relationship had survived a tragedy many couples didn't.

Recently, though, an emotional pressure had started building up inside him that continued to reach new levels and never abated. What had triggered it, he didn't know. David adapted to each increase and convinced himself this was as bad as it could get, only to have it worsen. His trick of half-listening (quarter-listening was more like it, or eighth-listening) no longer worked, and Jen's frequent lectures and soliloquies boosted the pressure like steam inside an old boiler.

Leaving her was out of the question. He would never summon the courage to broach the subject, and even if he had, he would have been shouted down before completing the first sentence. Their families were too interconnected for him to simply abandon her, his job, his life. That would require deserting his parents and siblings, too.

Which left the hair dryer in the bathtub, far simpler than untraceable exotic poisons or fatal vehicle accidents or all those other ways he'd read about in books.

David checked his watch. Over an hour since the blackout began. The radio announcers had run out of new things to say. Where had the time gone?

Should he go into the hall and pound on his neighbor's door? "Help, I think my wife's dead. Oh, please, help."

The words sounded unconvincing in his head. He couldn't bring himself to speak them aloud, afraid the lie, once established in his voice, would refuse to let go.

Preternatural silence filled the room, which was getting warm without AC. He didn't understand the logic behind Jen taking a steaming bath on a hot summer afternoon and then air conditioning the room down to arctic temperatures after she got out. However, the most courageous David ever got on the subject was to pointedly wear a sweater, which was either too subtle for his wife or she chose to ignore it.

Just leave, a voice inside his head repeated. Go downstairs, get lost among the crowds, live a little, experience the moment. Something like this only happens once a decade. Years from now people will be asking what you were doing when the lights went out. Have an interesting answer for a change. Don't sit in the apartment and then have nothing to offer when they ask.

He laughed gently. He already had an interesting answer, one he would never get to use. "When the power went out, I was electrocuting my wife." That brought an unaccustomed smile to his face, for the real answer was, "What was I doing? I *caused* the Blackout of 2003."

All the pressure that had been building inside him for days, weeks, months fell away. He could get through this. By now everyone who was going to leave the building already had, so the stairwell was probably empty. Thirty-eight flights down was freedom from this stuffy room and the claustrophobic life he'd lived within it for over a decade.

Downstairs, people were having a good time. A man in a business shirt was directing traffic to the applause of bystanders. Further down the street someone had opened up a fire hydrant and kids were playing in the gushing water. In Manhattan! Not in the Bronx, or Brooklyn, right here.

Then, later, after he'd shared communion with his neighbors, strangers unified by this event, one that he had caused, after all that he could return up the stairs–or maybe up the elevator if the power had returned, discover the horrifying scene in his bathroom and play the part of the grieving husband.

His coworkers would whisper about his terrible luck, first losing a child and now his wife. They'd smile at him in sympathy. He'd dress the way he wanted, pack his own damn suitcases, eat at Wendy's, and drive the car on streets of his choosing.

He opened the apartment door and breathed in the hallway's fresh air. A magnetic force tugged at him, drawing him out. "Come, play," it said. "Enjoy life again."

David drew more of the hallway air into his lungs and prepared to let the door close behind him when he heard a noise and turned.

His wife stood outside the bathroom door, wrapped in a towel.

"Where are you going, David? I've got a hellish headache, I'm sore all over and the lights won't come on. Get me a couple of Tylenol. Why is the power off? I think I fell asleep in the tub. Why didn't you wake me up? I'm cold. And I ruined my hair dryer. Didn't I tell you time and time again to move it away from the bathtub? Don't you know how dangerous that might have been? David? Are you listening to me? I need Tylenol."

David's body quickly returned to its old level of tension and escalated to new heights. He released the doorknob, let the door close in front of him, and turned back inside to find comfort for his wife.

Bev Vincent is a contributing editor with Cemetery Dance magazine and the author of over twenty short stories, including a recent contribution to Borderlands 5. His book THE ROAD TO THE DARK TOWER, an exploration of Stephen King's Dark Tower series, will be published by NAL in November 2004. (www.BevVincent.com)

GRAPHIC DESIGN

Tom Grimsby tossed the newspaper into the corner of the room with bored irritation.

"Bloody rubbish," he muttered. "Soaps and celebrities and football. And the paper's not even fit to wipe your arse on." The newspaper lay in a loosely crumpled heap on the floor. Nell would pick it up later, as she always did.

Tom shifted in his armchair, yawned and stretched his legs, oblivious of the two muddy furrows his boots had excavated in the carpet. He reached into his pocket for his tobacco pouch and rolled a cigarette, fresh tobacco spilling onto the tired upholstery of the chair to mix with the ash he dropped earlier.

Nell appeared in the doorway. She was wearing her usual nylon housecoat and her usual tired expression. Her hair was dusty grey and her eyes were dull and lifeless, a perfect match for her manner of defeated resignation. The only fresh thing about her appearance was the blue-black bruise on her left cheek.

"Your dinner will be ready in five minutes." She spoke in a flat tone, learned years ago in order to avoid antagonizing her husband. "So if you want to–you know– pay a visit, you'd better do it now."

Tom looked up, sharply. "I'll 'pay a visit' when I'm good

and ready woman. And not before!"

Nell took a step back. She knew that look.

Her husband recognized the little retreat as a gesture of submission and pressed his advantage. "You want to watch what you say and how you say it. Or you might get distracted and walk into another door." He clenched his fist to emphasize the point.

"I didn't mean any harm, Tom. I just don't want the dinner to get ruined. And you always go before your dinner—for your digestion." Nell, fearing she had said too much, took another step back toward the comfort of her kitchen.

"And where's the boy? How come your precious David isn't about to ruin your dinner?"

Nell took a deep breath. "He won't be home for dinner. He's gone to his interview at the university. Remember, the graphic design course." She paused, but her pride in her son made her continue, "You should be proud of him, Tom. He's worked so hard on that computer my sister gave him. You should see some of the stuff he can turn out."

Tom rose slowly from his chair. "I thought I had beaten that crazy idea out of him." He glared at his wife, "Unless, of course, someone replanted the seed! There will be no university. That's the end of it. Anyway, how is he supposed to travel thirty miles every day to get there? I'll be damned if I'm going to taxi him back and forth."

Nell whispered, "David's bought a little car. He saved the money from his summer job. He's got everything all worked out."

Tom strode towards the door, shouldering Nell out of the way. "Has he now? We'll see about that! He's still not too old for the belt, and his old man's still able to teach some discipline to the little queer!" He called back from the garden, "Five minutes! Make sure my dinner is on the table!"

He reached the end of the garden and stepped into the wooden privy. There had been a bathroom inside the house for the last fifteen years, but Tom was a traditionalist to his

core. Let the women and their little puppies pamper them-
selves in the 'little boys' room.' Tom still did his business
here, whatever the weather outside.

He fastened the catch on the door and undid his thick
leather belt. "Graphic designer," he muttered, before settling
on the wooden seat. "Over my dead body!"

Tom always viewed toilet tissue as a complete waste of
money and consequently he kept a constant supply of torn
newspaper hanging on a nail to the side of the aging toilet.
He favoured the local weekly–*The Echo*–as the paper wasn't
too shiny and usually not too black with newsprint. He pulled
a couple of pieces from the nail.

He tore a third remnant from the nail and hesitated. It felt
strange in his hand, not quite as soft as normal newspaper,
but also not like the supplements and flyers either. The headline was still intact:

"Freak accident kills sixty-two year old local man."

Tom puzzled over this for a moment. He always read
The Echo from cover to cover, and he was sure he did not
recall such an incident. He read on:

*"Local man Thomas Grimsby was tragically killed today
(26th June),"* Tom's mind was reeling with incomprehension
as he read on. *"In a freak accident which police described as
'a million-to-one chance,' Mr. Grimsby died instantly when
a car swerved to avoid a dog, careened out of control, crashed
through Mr. Grimsby's garden fence, and demolished the
household's outside lavatory. Unfortunately, Mr. Grimsby was
using the facilities at the time. The tragedy is further com-
pounded by the fact the car was driven by Mr. Grimsby's son,
David."*

Tom looked at the accompanying photograph with be-
wildered eyes. The grainy, black and white image showed a
car amongst the wreckage of shattered wood and debris. At
the top of the photograph was an inset picture of Tom himself, hair neatly combed, smiling, taken on his wedding day.

Compelled to read on, Tom focused on the page again:

"Mr. Grimsby is survived by his widow, Nell, and his son, David, who was unhurt in the tragedy. A police spokesperson said the family was devastated by the loss of their loved one. The accident occurred at approximately 1:15 pm."

Tom looked at his watch. June 26th, 1:15 pm.

He heard the screech of the tires followed by the splintering fence.

Understanding dawned a split second before the final impact. Tom remembered Nell's words, 'He's been working so hard on that computer. You should see some of the stuff he can turn out.'

Michael Learmond lives in North Wales, UK, with his wife Gill and his two children, Amy and Alex. He has had several stories published in anthologies and magazines through out the world. He started writing because it looked easy and continued to write when he found it wasn't.

Pat Dennis

ONE FOR THE ROAD

Jenkin's Service Station specialized in fixing unnecessary repairs on RVs driven by seniors. This fact, however,
was not noted on the station's billboards that dotted Inter-
state 80 in Nevada. The roadside advertising instead promised honest and friendly estimates, as well as a free gift with
every $19.95 oil change. The gift turned out to be a card-
board, strawberry-scented, cactus-shaped air freshener. The
oil change often turned into a $1,800 repair.

Al Jenkins had a new black Cadillac, five employees, and
a 24-year old receptionist whose Christmas bonus was a set
of silicone implants, extra large. So life, for Al, was very
good, and he was convinced it was about to get a whole lot
better.

"It's in pretty bad shape," Al said coming into the waiting room, his extra pounds creeping through his gray me-
chanic overalls. He wiped his hands on a filthy rag. If the
seventy-some-year-old Gundersons had better vision they
would have noticed something odd. The massive gold and
bejeweled ring on Al's hand was spotless. Al hadn't been
anywhere near an engine in years.

Mrs. Gunderson did not respond. She stood up, adjusted
her pink sweat suit that was embroidered gaily with hopping

and smiling bunnies, and stormed out of the shop, using every conceivable curse word along the way.

Mr. Gunderson shifted from side to side. "She misses the
grandkids." Then he added with a cold preciseness, "She hates
the motor home."

Al, nodded in understanding, "Most of 'em do.   See it
everyday."

Al himself did not have a wife, preferring instead an occasional visit to the Strawberry Cactus Brothel.   Of course
Al tried being married once but his young bride left him for
an old man with money. By now Al could barely remember
her name and found it odd that his mom would say, after her
daily quota of seven vodka gimlets, that her son never got
over his heartbreak. If anything, Al understood it made him
the man he was today. He was happy he found out early in
life what really mattered.

But Al knew that if he were still married he would not be
like the idiot husbands who came into his shop.

It was the husbands who dreamed of the Alaska wilderness, not the wives. It was the men who fantasized of driving
on ice-covered mountain roads as they narrowly escaped herds
of galloping moose. It was the men who insisted their cata-
ract covered eyes and rapidly slowing reflexes were a match
for any wilderness adventure.

And it was the women who insisted that if they had to
live in an RV then it damn well better be the same size of the
home they left behind.

By the time most of the RV couples reached Jenkin's Service Station, they were considering divorce, or murder.

"You headed to Alaska?"

Gunderson nodded, "How'd you know?"

Because all of you morons want to go there, Al wanted to
say. " The highways are filled with people with the same
dream."

"What did you say was wrong?   It seemed fine when we
drove it in."

"Didn't you notice it slowing down a bit when it went uphill?"

"Well, a little, of course, but that's...".

"You didn't hear the clinking? It's not that loud but if you're losing your hearing..."Al said, slowing down to a nice, loud, patronizing drawl.

"My hearing's fine. Of course I heard it," Gunderson answered as Al noticed the perplexed look on his face. Al could tell that Gunderson was the kind of man who would be too proud to admit any evidence of aging.

"It's the transmission and the brakes."

"God Almighty, how much is that gonna cost?"

"Well, it's a Sunday morning and my men are all in church," Al noted, "So to get them to come in, why that's time and a half right there and...".

"Geeze, what are we talking, a couple thousand here?" Gunderson asked, looking out the window towards his wife.

"At least," Al added, knowing by now the man was an easy take. Gunderson was more afraid of his wife then any car repair scam.

"Then I got a problem, a big one." Gunderson said, the weight of it all forcing him to sit down on the orange vinyl couch, right on top of the Reader's Digest magazine his wife had been reading.

"What is it?" Al asked, afraid he had misjudged the old coot's ability to pay. Al was convinced that most seniors had more money then they knew what to do with.

"Please, don't tell my wife, but I maxed out my credit cards in Las Vegas. I never had such a string of bad luck as I did in that town."

"I'll take a check," Al said wondering if he had to get rid of the old man how he would convince him the RV was suddenly safe to drive.

"Won't do you any good. Nothing's there, not until the first of the month when the checks arrive, and then that's not enough. Lord, I'm beginning to hate the RV myself. I don't care if I ever see Alaska. I just want to go back home."

Al looked through the grimy windows of his shop and stared at his real moneymaker, the Good Day Used RV Sales lot across the street.

"Well, I don't usually do this but I guess I could make you an offer. Of course the RV is kind of worn down, and…"

"It's only three years old."

"Well, then it's a three-year-old lemon," Al said, his voice softening. "It's a shame someone sold it to you. You'd think the government would protect our senior citizens more."

"I'm a Vet. Korea."

"I know. I saw the license plates. Listen, I can give you $8,000 in cash."

"But I paid $35,000 three years ago. It's gotta be worth more than that."

"You know what they say, the value drops as soon as you drive it off the lot. And you've put on mileage, and with the transmission and all…"

"Dolores is going to kill me. I told her I gambled thirty dollars."

"Don't tell her anything yet. Wait till you get home. Just tell her you're sick of the road and you want to see your grandkids."

"I bet she'd believe that," Gunderson said, and then with a loud sigh, "All you can go is eight?"

"Well, I guess I can give you ten. Tell you what, I'll even let you borrow my Caddy."

Gunderson's eyes lit up. "You'll let me drive your Cadillac to Minnesota?"

"No, just the forty miles to Elko. Just park it in the Stockmen's Casino parking lot, toss the keys under the front seat and lock it. I'll have one of my men pick it up tomorrow. There's at least five charter flights a day heading to Vegas from Elko. You can catch a plane home from there. "

"I don't know…"

Al went in for the kill. "Besides, with $10,000 in your pocket, your luck's gonna change. With that kind of dough you could hit it big in Vegas, and you'd never have to tell the little woman what you did."

"You have no idea how nice that would be," Gunderson said, looking out towards the parking lot where Dolores was simultaneously chain smoking and eating a candy bar. "She's a good woman but she does have a temper."

"You got the registration and the title?"

"That's another problem."

"What do you mean?" Al asked, totally frustrated. If the deal fell through, he would have wasted an entire morning. He could have spent it instead at the brothel, like most of his employees.

"Let's go inside and I'll show you."

Al and Gunderson entered the twenty-foot RV, and Gunderson led him to the tiny bathroom, complete with sink, chemical toilet, and a showerhead on the far right side of the wall. Taped on the wall, directly across from the showerhead, was a water soaked vehicle title that was no longer readable.

"I thought it would decorate the bathroom. And I could look at it every time I sat down and remember how lucky I was to be on the road instead of working at the factory. Now you can barely read it, most of the ink's washed off. I guess we could call the motor vehicle place but it being Sunday…".

Al looked at the ruined title on the wall. It was further proof that old people should not be allowed on the road.

"I can take care of it. Just take it down and sign it over. I have friends at the DMS. If there's a problem, I'll get a hold of you in Minnesota."

Gunderson reached over and gently pulled the title off the wall. "It's amazing, isn't it?" Gunderson asked, "How much they can put in these tiny bathrooms. You got everything in here a man could need, including an air freshener. I guess it's a deal then. Should we shake on it?"

"Sure," Al answered, amused that he was clinching a deal

in an RV bathroom that would net him an easy $15,000 profit.

Al waited as Gunderson slowly exited the RV. Al smiled as he walked the small aisle, noting oak walls, a sparkling microwave, a DVD player and monitor. "Sweet," he mumbled to himself, "sweet."

"We gotta' get our stuff out of here," Gunderson remembered at the bottom of the RV steps.

"And I've got to give you your money," Al answered.

Gunderson laughed. "I almost forgot about that. My memory's not as good as it use to be."

Good thing, Al thought to himself. By next week Gunderson would even forget he owned an RV.

"My safe's in the office." Al led Gunderson to his office, a small room off the mechanics' area. The room was paneled in simulated pine. A walnut veneer desk was piled high with papers and empty beer cans. Al leaned down and opened the safe.

"I don't usually keep this much on hand," Al said, not admitting that he did most repairs in cash to avoid paying taxes. "But, I haven't got to the bank yet."

Al pulled out a stack of hundreds. "You need to fill out some forms. Got your driver's license?'

"You need that?"

"Now what? Don't tell me..."

"I think I left it at Circus-Circus but I got the number written down. I always carry a list of all my numbers: Social Security, drivers license, address, and my AARP number. You need my AARP number?"

Al looked at him. If it were anyone else the deal would have ended right there, but Al was convinced the old man was telling the truth. Al had never met such a scatterbrain. He felt his blood pressure rise as he realized he could have gotten the RV for eight grand if he only pressed it.

"Just fill out these forms," Al said as he watched the old man squint through bifocals to read the papers. Gunderson opened his worn leather wallet and pulled out a list of numbers that were written on a tiny scrap of paper.

Al noticed only two or three small bills in Gunderson's wallet. That was all he had. He almost felt sorry for the old guy but stopped himself short. As far as Al was concerned, he had just lost $2,000 on the deal.

Al helped the Gundersons empty the RV. It was amazing how little they had. Dolores insisted on holding the framed photos of the grandkids, and the rest went into the Cadillac's trunk. Al filled the gas tank and gave them written instructions on how to get to Elko.

"If you make the right connections, you can be back in Minnesota for dinner," Al told them as he closed the door and handed Gunderson the keys. "You could even have one of those smorgasbords I heard about."

"You betcha," said Gunderson smiling. He started the engine and waved goodbye as he drove twenty miles an hour down the highway. It was ten minutes before the car was out of sight, then he floored it and reached his preferred eighty miles an hour.

"He paid in cash?" the little woman asked, looking at the framed photos in her hand.

"Ten grand."

"Idiot," she answered as she changed the radio station from easy listening to heavy metal. " Why did you say my name was Dolores? You know I hate that name."

" It sounded like a Minnesota name," said Gunderson, whose real name was Schwartz. He took off the bifocals and tossed them out the window. "You wanted me to tell him your real name, Sue?"

"Of course not, but it could have been a nicer name. I like the name Roberta. Use that next time," Sue said, throwing the framed photos of somebody's grandkids along the side of the highway. "How long do you think it will take this one to realize the RV's hot?"

"Twenty-four hours at least. That's why we do business on a Sunday."

"We'll be back in L.A. by then for sure. You know someone who'll buy the Caddy?"

"Are you kidding? At my age, I know everything."

Pat Dennis is the author of HOTDISH TO DIE FOR—a collection of culinary mystery short stories. She is the recipient of the Midwest Independent Publisher's Association Merit Award for Fiction for her novel STAND-UP AND DIE. Pat works as a humorist and is often mistaken for a motivational speaker, which she is not. She just likes to talk loudly in public and be paid for it. Pat is the Creative Director of Penury Press. (www.penurypress.com)

Kevin Carollo

CHARLIE AND ME

I know how to hide in small places. It's because I'm small that I can do it. My mom and me, we live in a tiny apartment that costs too much. But even in a small apartment there are places to hide. I don't have to pay right now because Mom wins the bread for us. When she leaves for work, she says, "Amanda, I'm going to win the bread for us. Be careful." She doesn't see me when she says this. I am hiding. Like a cat.

When Mom goes to the mansions, sometimes I go with. There I get to see "how the other half lives," Mom says. For your information, the other half have kitchens and bathrooms just like us, only much bigger. Lots of cupboards, many places to hide—if you are tiny like me. The other half like to have bathrooms on every floor. I was in the upstairs bathroom when the old man was killed in it. No one saw me. But I can tell you something. I was under the sink the whole time.

It is fun to play hide and seek, even by yourself. Eventually someone comes looking. You have to be really quiet. Even small people can get in the way. This I have learned the hard way. When the old man was killed, it was with a gun. Not the kind that goes "pow," but one that is real quiet, a gun that goes "pfft." Three times. I heard him fall into the shower, even though someone had turned the air on. I was real scared, so I stayed quiet like the gun.

My mom, she works in a bookstore. But when we go to the mansions, it's so she can tell the other half how much money their rugs and vases and fancy books cost. My mom and me like books too. I've been reading books all my life. At least as long as I can remember. Mom is good at her job, but it can take a good while to win the bread. I don't get too bored, as long as I'm allowed to investigate. By "investigate," I mean hiding. Then seeing what others don't make time to see.

Some time after the old man was shot with the quiet gun, my mom started calling out to me. "Amanda, we have to leave now! It's time to go, calico," she said. She calls me that because we had a calico cat once. Louise. She liked to sleep under the kitchen sink. Anyway, when Mom called me, I wanted to tell her where I was. But I didn't dare. The killer had left, but you know how they sometimes come back to the scene of the crime. So I kept good and quiet for a good long time.

Then someone came into the bathroom. Someone from staff. She spoke Spanish, and it sounded like crying. I know how to say "Me llamo Amanda. Como está?" I'm learning Spanish in school. But this time I wasn't about to practice any Spanish. I had to wait and see what would happen.

Pretty soon a bunch of people came in. Someone called for a doctor. Basically, the other half went frantic, as my mom would say. I heard many voices shouting at each other, men and women, Spanish and English, old and young. And the whole time Mom was calling "Amanda! Amanda!" out to me. She was going frantic too. I wanted to shout, "I'm okay!" back at her, but I was too afraid to go peep.

Here's what happened before all the commotion. After the gun went "pfft, pfft, pfft," and after I counted real slow to 33—my favorite number—I took a small peek. I saw the old man next to the cloudy glass door of the shower. He wore a black suit, and his legs hung outside the shower in the air. He had fancy shoes on. "Wingtips", they call them. He seemed far away, because it's a big bathroom, and because I only opened the door a sliver. I had to let my ears do the seeing for the most part.

Nothing moved. The old man looked like Alfred Hitchcock, who I once heard on TV say that he didn't like showers. I can see why. Gold trim was everywhere, framing the cloudy bald head of the old man. Some blood, I suspected, but not as much as in the movies. There was a big throw rug underneath his big feet. It was a kind of orange that had some red in it.

So, all in all, I didn't see too much from under the sink. But I heard a lot more, before all the commotion and frantic started. After the gun was fired, the person didn't just leave. The person with the gun waited until I was at 14 before leaving, and I was counting slow as I could. Then Charlie—that's what I call the killer—then Charlie put his hands over the sink, right above my head, and turned on the water. I heard it flow down the pipe right next to me.

Charlie didn't want to wash his hands. I bet he was wearing gloves so his fingertips wouldn't be all over the place. So why did he turn on the water? I wonder. Then Charlie whispered a bad word, and reached down for something that dropped. I thought it might be a piece of jewelry, or maybe a silver dollar. I only realized exactly what it was later. Just that small thing and the cupboard door separated Charlie and me. I kept hush as tight as I could, because Charlie knew I was there. He must've.

Charlie picked up the tiny thing, then left. The shoes Charlie wore made a "shush shush" sound, like a feather duster. And then that was all I heard for awhile. Not even my own breath. I never saw what Charlie looked like. But he kinda sounded like he was in a hurry and taking his time. Some things just don't make sense.

When the policemen came in, I waited some more. They were "casing the joint," as they say on TV. They would find me soon. When they finally did, I came out. Mom found me and started crying. I started crying too, because I saw her all frantic with tears. Like she was the one time I got lost in the supermarket. That was a long time ago though, when I was very young.

For a long time, I had to stay near the policewoman. She said she was a sort of social worker, and wanted to make sure I was okay to socialize with people. Everyone at the mansion had to stay put while the police searched the whole mansion. There were the maids, the cooks, and all the staff. There were the sons and daughter, the accountants, and the other half guests. Like a ball. Or the opera.

The sons all had brownish-red hair, and the daughter had red-red hair. I know all this because everybody had to say who they were and why they were there and what time it was that everything happened. For the moment, I just watched. The maid who found the body only spoke Spanish. Now I saw her outfit, saw what exactly she looked like when she was at work. She said a bunch of words like "horror" and "terror," but in Spanish. You roll the Rs. This is called a trill. All of the other half guests were in suits and dressing gowns. No one touched the books or drank from their drinks.

My mom was composing herself, trying not to lose it over and over again. She and the social worker told me more about the old man, why my mom was there for work, and filled me in on the details. I kinda knew some of the stuff already, some not. The old man was rich, the richest of all the other half. This job would have paid our rent for a few months, Mom said. Then she repeated what she told me—more or less—to the police. No one really asked me any questions then, but I could tell that people were starting to look at me in a funny kind of way.

Is she okay to talk? asked a policeman.

Let me ask her, okay? asked my mom back. I said I was okay, only without speaking. We have a secret code.

At that point in time, everyone was milling around, sort of like Louise used to when she wanted to be fed. They paid me too much attention. I looked at some of them back, but tried hard to stay mum. It was too much, all these people. Then I said kinda loud, "I know how the old man was killed."

No one said anything after that. They just listened. They were in disbelief. People stared at me, the tiny girl who had been under the bathroom sink the whole time. After awhile— I counted to five in Spanish—a policeman said to me, "You can tell us, Amanda." He spoke gentle, like a relative would, maybe. But I had never seen him before. I kept going.

"There were three shots." Everyone wondered what I was going to say next, including myself. I'm not used to socializing. I raised my voice even more.

"The old man fell into the shower. He made a thump."

Their faces began to turn sour, like they were on their way to the dentist.

"Charlie—the person with the gun —dropped that pin that holds the shirt together."

"Cuff links, honey," said my mom in her it's-going-to-be-okay voice.

"Then he said a bad word."

Some of them smiled at me. The policeman added, "You don't have to say the word, Amanda." They even laughed a little after he said this. I smiled for a second. But I had to keep talking.

"Charlie is in this room," I said. You can bet they stopped laughing just then.

"Charlie wears soft shoes. Like slippers."

The policeman asked me to explain.

"The kind that go 'shush shush' when you walk on expensive rugs." I had heard that kind of sound before. Usually when hiding at other mansions.

"That means there can only be one Charlie." At this point

in time, Mom had a real look of *horror* and *terror* on her face.

No one breathed a breath. Not one sigh.

"He's the one with loose cuff links and feather duster shoes."

I had finished my story. But I still had to point Charlie out to everyone.

I aimed my pointer finger to the right, to the man with one cuff link on. I pointed to the youngest son of the dead old man.

Charlie was the youngest brother.

They took him away soon after. When they questioned everyone, they found out Charlie thought the old man forgot to put him in the will. True or not, this is called motive. He tried to keep hush about it too, but I think my guess is pretty good. You could see it on his face. Everyone could.

It so happens that Charlie was in the will after all. He was even going to make a lot of money. But somehow he came to doubt things. It made him furious, because he felt the older brothers were always the old man's favorites. Something like that. I stop paying attention after awhile. The other half is never satisfied.

All I know is he made the same "shush shush" sound across the den's Persian rug. The same kind that's in the bathroom. Each cuff link had a tiny velvet flower. They found one in his shirt where it belongs, and one in his pocket. No one else had one cuff link on, at least as far as I could tell.

It takes longer to know what happened than it takes for it to happen. Now I've learned this the hard way. Maybe I jumped to conclusions too fast. But there is compensation money for Mom and me if I've jumped to the right one. Either way, we'll get by. For the meanwhile, Mom decided to treat us to our favorite Mexican restaurant. Everyone there helps me practice Spanish. I tell them "por favor" and "gracias" for the food.

That's the story pretty much, the story of Charlie and me. Look hard and you might see me. I'll be hiding. No more mansions for a while. Maybe a cat. Perhaps another calico.

Kevin Carollo received his Ph.D. in comparative literature from the University of Illinois. He currently teaches world literature in the English Department at Minnesota State University Moorhead, and contributes regular book reviews to *Rain Taxi*. For some reason, he constantly dreams of calico cats named Louise and charcoal-gray cats named Harold.

David Dumitru

WASH AND WEAR

Dolores loathed the suits and the way he wore them. Wash and wear from the Suit'nSave. Off the rack, ill fitting, and crumpled just so in just the right places. They were his trial suits, she knew, meant to play to the jury, to make Beaux Holliday – Mr. Call Me Bo – look like some cornpone country lawyer, a man of the people. Even that unruly cowlick that stuck out from the top of his head like a rooster comb was a fake. A weave and Dolores knew it.

The judge cleared his throat and ruffled a stack of papers for effect. Dolores' attention had been fixed on a coffee-colored stain on the cuff of Holliday's right pant-leg. "Ms. Benevides," said the judge, "does the State have any questions for the witness?"

Dolores shot up from her seat at the prosecutor's table, straightened her knee-length skirt, and smoothed the lapels of her jacket–Saks in Dallas, two hundred and fifty dollars on sale. Dolores respected the sanctity of the courtroom during a murder trial and dressed accordingly. The contrast between herself and Holliday was stark. Trial masks, high theatre, and the Art of War, is how she thought of it. Off duty, she was a flower-pattern sundress girl; he, Armani and hand-tooled boots from over in Fort Worth.

"Thank you, Your Honor," she began. She spoke to the

bench while shooting glances at the jury box. "I must have been distracted, no, shocked, at the thought that this witness could sit there under oath and say the exact opposite of everything he told the police..."

Holliday rose up half-way in his seat and emitted a loud, weary sigh. His hands were splayed on the defense table and one of them slipped as he spoke, knocking a legal pad onto the floor and jarring the water pitcher that sat between him and his client. "I'm sorry, Judge Hanes," he said. "But I'm going to have to object." He sighed again and sucked in a large volume of air so that his larynx rattled with the effort. His eyelids slid closed for a second as if he were struggling to overcome a nervous tic of some kind. Finally, he started up again. "My esteemed colleague over here, the people's attorney, is testifying, Your Honor. And while I am fascinated with her opinions..."

"Objection sustained," Judge Hanes said.

But Holliday wasn't finished. He ambled on. "Now if Ms. Benevides would like to take the stand, I would be more than happy to assist her in getting to the bottom of what ails her..."

"Enough," said the judge. "Counsel for the State will save her comments for closing argument."

Dolores took a steadying breath and turned to the witness. She knew enough to know without looking that Holliday would be admiring her legs and the curve of her breasts, taking care not to let the jury see, but doing it all the same. It was well-known in courthouse circles that more than one assistant D.A. had lost her job by falling for his folksy mannerisms and then falling into his bed. Dolores, for her own part, knew better. She knew things the others did not and was not about to compromise her career.

"Mr. Tascoli," she said. "Did you not tell the police that you saw Mr. Havascomb come out of the restroom at the Bag 'n Go at about 3 PM on January the 3rd of this year? And did you not tell the police that after he left, you went into the restroom and found the deceased, Billy Mack Oakman, dead?

With his head in the toilet? Drowned?"

The witness shifted in his chair and pinched the end of his bony nose. His eyes darted from the jury to the defense table and back to Dolores in a bout of nervous calculation. "I don't know from drowned," he drawled. "Looked to me like he mighta been prayin'."

There was a spate of tittering from the jury box. Not a good sign. Before Dolores could stop him, heartened by the reaction of his audience, Tascoli added, "Prayin' or pukin', take yer pick."

He snickered through yellow, broken teeth at his own alliterative genius.

Dolores put one foot behind the other and took a dignified step back, her eyes drilling into Tascoli's. "A man's dead here, Mr. Tascoli," she chastened. "It's no laughing matter."

Apparently, Dolores was wrong on this point. Her jaw went taught when she saw the judge hunkered down in his chair, hiding his face behind a stack of motions and pleas, giggling.

Tascoli leaned forward in the witness box, taking advantage of her silence. "Never seen a man praying with his pants down around his ankles before, though, hairy little butt stickin' up in the air that'a way."

The judge fell sideways in his chair. Several jurors guffawed. Others, the older ladies for the most part, covered their mouths with both hands, both embarrassed and amused.

"Your Honor!" Dolores nearly shouted. At last the gavel came down on top of the bench, and Judge Hanes called the room to order.

Dolores spent the next several minutes trying to recover the momentum, to no avail. Tascoli was not going to budge. Havascomb, the defendant, had gotten to him some how, some way. A bribe or a threat, it didn't matter which from Dolores' point of view. And Holliday most likely knew it or suspected as much. She gave him a look that she hoped was a glare, and saw him looking back at her with that hangdog expression, as if to say, "All's fair in love and war" and this, my dear, is an instance of the latter. She gave up trying to poke holes in Tascoli's story and excused him from the stand.

In an attempt at rehabilitating the memory of the deceased Billy Mack Oakman, Dolores shuffled her notes again and called Billy Mack's mother as a witness.

"Mrs. Oakman," Dolores started with all the sympathy she could muster.

Billy Mack's mother interrupted, gripping the microphone with three-inch, neon-blue fingernails. "I don't go by that name no more," she corrected.

"Oh, excuse me," Dolores replied, taken aback. She re-checked her Victim Interview notes then raised her eyes again to face the witness. "But..."

"I got married again, just after Billy Mack died. Thank God," Billy Mack's mother said. "I was just a'waitin' fer him to kick off, you know. He tolt me if'n I ever got myself married agin, he'd a' kilt me dead."

Dolores checked her notes for a third time. She would, before the day was out, flay the Victim Interview Specialist who had supposedly prepped the witness. "No further questions," she said, slipping into her seat.

"Kin I go now?" Billy Mack's mother asked the judge with a flirtatious, white-gloss lipstick smile.

The judge nodded, but then jerked his head back and to the side at Holliday's "Uh, hem. I have a few questions for the witness, Your Honor. If you don't mind."

Holliday gave the witness his warmest smile as if thanking her in advance for another win at trial. He asked, "Billy Mack didn't want you marrying again? So you had a motive to kill him yourself, did you not?"

"Hell," Billy Mack's mother said. She patted the side of her bleached beehive to keep it straight on her head, adding, "I'da done it, sure. Who wouldn't? He was no good." She wasn't finished and Holliday let her go on. "A mother tries, you know." Her eyes welled up now, her purple mascara threatened to run. "He didn't have no beer or cigarettes 'til he was ten, you know. Not in *my* house anyways. And no strong spirits until he reached twelve years old." She sniffed, a wet and viscous sound that made its way down her throat, then hocked and swallowed. "I'm sorry," she sobbed, "I just can't go on…"

Holliday said "No further questions," and the judge excused her from the stand.

Dolores turned a baleful eye in the direction of the defense table. Havascomb poured water from the pitcher into a glass and smiled as he drank. Holliday grinned at her and poured another glass of water for his client when Havascomb had finished the first. Closing arguments took all of ten minutes. Dolores tried again to remind the jury that just because the deceased was a bad man was no excuse to set a killer free. Havascomb himself was no barrel of apples, she said. A drug dealer, a known felon, a wife beater, and most likely a child molester to boot. Holliday could have objected to the vast majority of what she argued, she knew, but he held his tongue.

When it was his turn, Holliday merely reiterated the evidence and relied on the old Texas standby defense–his personal stock-in-trade. Billy Mack, he implied, was a man in need of a good killin'. If indeed Havascomb had done the deed, it was in the spirit of community service. Just ask Billy's own mother. At the end of arguments, the jury filed out, the jury foreman even tipping his hand in salute to Holliday's brevity.

Out in the hallway Dolores found Holliday and Havascomb sitting together on a low bench along the wall. Havascomb was rocking back and forth, holding his stomach in a nervous clinch but still able to muster a sneer for the prosecutor. Dolores said, "That was below even you, Counselor. Suborning perjury that way. You know Tascoli was lying through his teeth."

"Do I, now?" Holliday said. He drew himself up to his usual height, abandoning the hokey slouch he affected in court.

The trial mask was sliding off.

Havascomb rose from his seat and excused himself, saying, "Gotta go see a man about a load a' bricks."

Dolores watched him go, crabbing to one side, clutching his mid-section on his way to the restroom. She eyed Holliday again, her own trial persona still intact. "What you won't do to win," she scoffed, shaking her head.

"What I won't do," he echoed.

Dolores turned and went back to her office to await the verdict. There was still a chance of a guilty verdict. Juries tend to convict a person, no matter the evidence, if they wouldn't feel comfortable riding down the elevator with them after the trial – an elevator verdict, it was called. Havascomb, with his idiotic swagger and empty, leering eyes, was a prime candidate for such a verdict.

Fifteen minutes later the jury was back. They had taken even that long, it was discovered, because one of ladies had needed to a restroom break. Judge Hanes scanned the room and announced, "Mr. Holliday, where's your client?"

Holliday rose and said, "I'm not sure, Your Honor. I expect he'll be along in a minute."

As he sat back down there was a bustle and a murmur in the courtroom as a bailiff came rushing up the aisle and up to the bench. He was out of breath, and the cuffs of his pants were dripping wet, oozing water onto the carpet. "It's Havascomb, Judge," he panted. "He's dead. In the restroom. Got his head stuck in a commode."

The sound in the courtroom grew louder as people nudged each other, sharing their shock and surprise. The Bailiff went on. "We got the courthouse sealed off, but it looks like whoever done it got clean away."

Judge Hanes hammered away with his gavel while observers scattered, heading out through the nearest doors. Holliday sat in his chair, watching, his gaze fixed on the judge. After a moment he called out over the din, "Judge, can we at least hear the verdict?"

Hanes looked to the jury foreman and sent him a solemn nod. The foreman took a slip of paper out of his pocket and shouted, "Not guilty."

Holliday looked over at Dolores. She rolled her eyes at him and started packing her briefcase. "Win some, lose some," she said as she passed him on the way out.

He jerked to his feet, knocking the table with his knees as he did, and called after her. She stopped and turned and watched him scramble to save the pitcher of water from spilling once again. Water sloshed everywhere; the pitcher toppled, Holliday's shoes were soaked, as were the cuffs of his pants. There was water seeping up the sleeves of his jacket. He pulled a handkerchief from an inside pocket to dry his hands. The handkerchief he discarded in trash can next to the table. He shook his head at his own clumsiness and then leveled his gaze on her. "Dinner? Tonight?"

She took a step toward him and raised her free hand as if to pluck his eyeballs from his head. She surveyed the courtroom for eavesdroppers and said, "I cannot believe you just said that, right here, right now."

The clock beside Dolores' bed ticked and tocked. She stared at it, unable to sleep. After this one, her third loss against Holliday, she doubted her career was on what anyone would call a fast-track. A hand slipped over the calf of her right leg and slid up her thigh, caressing and gently prodding as it went.

"Come into practice with me," Holliday said. "You could do worse."

She took his hand and squeezed, ignoring the suggestion. "How many is that?" she asked. "Five?"

"Six," he said, "counting Billy Mack."

"He was a client?"

"Not yet," he answered, "But it was only a matter of time. A man like him, bound to kill somebody some day, end up on my doorstep wanting me to get him off. Like I said at trial, he was a man in need of a killin."

"You set it up so Havascomb would find Billy Mack," she said. "You knew he'd run, which would make him look guilty, and then have to pay you to defend him."

"That I did. He needed a good killin' himself. And he paid me for it too."

"Did he bribe Tascoli?"

"That would be unethical."

"Unethical," Dolores purred. She yawned. "So how? Havascomb?"

"Laxative," he answered, a yawn in sympathy with hers expanding his chest against her back. "In the water, so I knew he'd have the trots during jury deliberations. I just followed him in there and did him. A man in the throes of a diarrhea attack won't put up much of a fight. Smells like hell, but can't fight worth a God damn."

"The water, you spilled it after the trial."

"Evidence," he said.

"The water on your jacket and pants," she said.

"Wash and wear," he said. "Had to wash his filth off after I did him."

Dolores turned over and kissed him on the cheek. She dropped her head down on her pillow and closed her eyes, half asleep.

"Wash and wear," she said.

"And on sale," he said.

David Dumitru is a stay-at-home dad and writer in St. Louis, MO. Between trips to Office Depot for printer cartridges for his manuscripts, he enjoys writing about himself in the third person and chasing silverfish around in the basement. To the best of his recollection, he once pursued a career as a drummer and practiced criminal defense law in Texas. He is currently recovering from a five-year sojourn in Australia, where he learned to say g'day mate and consume meat pies.

R.J. Mills

PORT-O-PRINCE

The Daily News crisscrossed the detective room like a pre-dawn delivery truck, behind schedule, and running hot. Paper fluttered from desks and gathered in his wake as the loudmouth rookie of the 14th precinct scanned the room. My partner, nicknamed after New York's patron saint of misinformation, was constantly seeking my attention. I was rarely entranced.

My eyes bounced between the headline decrying another looming transit strike and my partner. For the moment, age and the state of my lower G.I. had me sympathetic with jammed up tunnels, but D.N. seemed capable of that on a more regular basis.

He neared, and I raised the paper an inch, sliding further behind in eating my bagel. Daily News suited him, but I called him D.N. for short. It reminded me of the writer's last words: The End. Anyone subjected to his know-it-all summations would agree it was an appropriate moniker, fitting him like his pants, skintight.

The trouble? I saw my remaining months on the force as a kind of real world "Survivor" episode: stay out of trouble, avoid transfer and bullets with my name on them. So far, since leaving Manhattan North, I'd kept my record clean, and over-confidant or not, I canceled my U-Haul reservation. Now, if I could only lose the limp.

But trouble and I had a way of finding each other, and the slug in my hip ached as it and D.N. worked painfully over pressure points. And hoofing it after drugged out punks through Washington Square Park didn't help. He didn't understand that I wasn't Eddie "Popeye" Doyle from French Connection fame, not that I ever was.

As far as partners went though, I had to admit, D.N. was one of the best. And I've had too many to count, in precincts from the battery up to the famed Fort Apache in the Bronx. The latest snot-nose bounced toward me. I hoped I could survive his enthusiasm.

Johnny "Fats" Demarco stabbed a bratwurst-looking finger in my direction. I winced and made a mental note to slip a piece of Ex-Lax into one of his Yoo-Hoos. My stakeout exposed, I lowered the paper and swept the half-eaten bagel off into the garbage can. I crushed the grease-stained benefits letter I'd used as a paper plate. Congratulating myself for avoiding lectures on heart disease and early retirement I muttered, "The End."

"Hey, man, I been looking all over for you. Where you been, huh?" His thin, curving sideburns looked like human graffiti drawn on brownstone walls. The smell of cumin rode a wave ahead of him.

I held my hands out, and he stopped. "Funny," I said, "I always seem to be in the last place you look. Don't I?"

Either missing the sarcasm or ignoring it, he said, "Hey, forget it; I got us a good case, man. Let's go." He turned and walked toward the watch supervisor's office. Through yellowed blinds I could see several black suits conferring with the lieutenant.

I felt the leash tighten and forced my balled-up fist to open. The crumpled letter dropped into the can. I yelled, "Hey, what's going on?"

D.N. beamed. "Man, this is good. A dude over in HR got popped. It's ours." He waved impatiently. "Come on, this one's gonna make the news for sure."

I hesitated to say it already had. "Hold on there, Tonto," I said. I needed to think; someone from Human Resources being killed meant the visitors were from internal affairs.

D.N. shrugged, then confirmed. "What else, man." He drew a pointed finger across his throat. "Someone goes p-f-f-f-t in the department, those guys get involved. Right?"

He didn't say it, but I heard it: "The End."

I pushed myself out of the chair. It groaned sympathetically. D.N. narrowed his eyes at me, and I asked defiantly, "What?" He pointed to my chin. "You got some cream cheese. . . *right* there." The End.

I stepped out of the Taurus and into a pile of dog crap at Lido and Son's salvage yard. I yelped, "Aghhhh!" and looked for a scraper, settling for the chrome fender of a car old enough to have one. The silvery reflection transformed the dingy yard with squat toilets into turreted castles and bulbous onion domes. D.N.'s distorted image waited impatiently.

"Chomping at the bit?" I said, "Take a look around back, then meet me in the office." I pointed my chin at the aluminum trailer with the chipped, wooden company sign. D.N. nodded and walked around the side of the building. A dog barked, and I grimaced at my shoe before looking back to The News. The IA guys, and the all-too-familiar smell had me wishing I was somewhere else.

They'd played the usual tune: keep it in the family, be discrete. I yessed them to death and got the hell out of there before I puked. I wouldn't miss the incestuous protection, the cover-ups. I'd bury the whole mess, including one or two of my own, on an isolated, foam-splashed stretch of island beach in the Caribbean. I closed my eyes and vowed, "Soon."

The challenge of the case was intriguing though, and I was convinced I could solve it. I'd then slide into retirement, for once smelling like a rose. I rolled my foot over. Satisfied,

I walked to the office, remembering Sharples's rundown of the case.

Like D.N. said, a human resources employee *had* been murdered. But the Lieutenant added something interesting. The body had been found in a portable toilet by a construction guy wanting to take a dump before zipping back home to Jersey.

The problem? Before a cop could arrive and secure the scene, an embarrassing thing happened. The toilet disappeared, with the body presumably still entombed. Moving a dead body before the coroner's office had a peek was a no-no. The compromised crime scene made the case like a floating crap game for the D.A. I smiled, sure that would become a gem among the other puns sure to do the locker room rounds.

So I took on the case, and here we were, at the headwaters of traveling toilets, two and a half hours after the report first came in from ground zero. I interviewed and D.N. watched, hopefully learning something. I leaned on the guy a little hard, but sometimes you learn stuff being hard on jamokes. Like that personnel guy who lost months of my timesheets.

Anyway, I was convinced the hardhat told us the truth. I asked, "Can you give me a description, sir?" He looked up. His eyes narrowed as if trying to see through a fog and said, "Around fifty; dark suit—maybe gray—"

"No," I said, "I mean the crapper. Do you remember what *it* looked like?" He looked incredulous, and I explained. "Mr. Costigan, we have a handle on the deceased. We have to find the crime scene. Capice?" He shook his head but gave us a good enough description to eliminate the other two of three suppliers contracted by the city. Lido and Sons had been a match.

I paused before pushing open the door at the top of rotting, wooden stairs. A man, so unhealthy looking he made *me* feel good, turned around at the noise. His swivel chair begged for mercy under three hundred pounds plus weight.

He smirked and nodded. "You the cop that called? I hear you need a toilet."

I nodded. "One in particular, actually."

The man had rows of flesh on his forehead that seemed contiguous with his wavy, red hair. Little Lotta smiled. "Don't ascribe to the any-port-in-a-storm philosophy, huh?"

I looked over his shoulder and through the window to the yard beyond. D.N. was making his way back toward the office, a long row of identical Port-O-Johns he'd checked behind him. He held a handkerchief to his nose. He looked pale. "Cute, Mr. Lido. You got the records you were asked for?"

"The News" entered, his black tie loose at his throat. Lido snorted and leaned back to retrieve a clipboard from the credenza. Amazingly, the chair held up, and he handed over the morning's manifests.

I flipped through the documents as Lido addressed D.N. "Hey, kid, you look like you need a drink. Want a milkshake?" The muscles in D.N.'s throat convulsed, but he regained control. Wiping his forehead, he said, "I'm fine, thanks."

Lido laughed. "Oh, yeah? Well, you should come back in the summer when it's nice and hot."

I felt sorry for the kid and tapped the sheaf of dog-eared papers to get Jabba the Jerk's attention. "According to these the toilet we're looking for was retrieved this morning, but there's no indication as to where it went."

Lido blew out sarcastically and shrugged. "And we're supposed to record where each crapper is at any given time? You think this is a homeland security hot spot or something?" He ran a meaty hand through his hair. I glowered at him and he softened, but the stiff curls sprung immediately back into place.

He knew the drill: screw with me, he gets regular visits from the Board of Health. "Look all you want," he said, jabbing a thick thumb over his shoulder to where D.N. had been checking. "All the returns are out there. They haven't been emptied yet, so if what you're looking for is in one of them, it's still there. Knock yourself out."

I slid the clipboard across Lido's desk and it bounced off his gut, ending the interview. I made for the door, preferring the smell outside to the acid stink of the closed office. I was about to close it and Lido called out. "Hey, Van Ider, you lose a Rolex in one of them?"

Glaring, I nodded and said, "Could be, wise ass. Want to go bobbing for apples?"

He waved me off with a meaty hand and picked up The Daily News's word scramble. The tortured chair screamed as he returned to stasis.

Despite the cloying scent of urinal sanitizer cakes, I breathed easier on the outside. But something that Lido said bothered me. Was it the Rolex comment, the inference that an honest cop shouldn't have one? I wasn't sure, but stored it away for the time being; we had a labyrinth of lavatories to check out.

I slapped D.N. on the back. "Come on, kid. There's no business like show business."

Twenty minutes, and a ton of checked toilets later, D.N. and I stood before the last two unchecked potties. I nodded, and he flipped the door latch with his pencil. The door banged open against the last remaining toilet, mine. Like a kid peeking into Santa's sack, D.N. looked inside, anticipation etched on his face. Disappointment replaced excitement. He looked to me and shook his head.

"Go ahead, man," he said, mustering as much positive energy as he could, "this bust's for you."

I gave him a Boy Scout salute then opened the last door. A part of me hated to disappoint D.N.; he seemed so sure we'd find the body. And I felt bad for busting him, for going along with the rest of the squad. But he was, after all, a rookie; dues had to be paid. "Sorry, kid," I said as I closed the Port-o-Potty, "better luck next time."

I put my arm around his shoulder, meaning to guide him back to the car. But he remained planted in front of the last toilet. I laughed, asking, "What is it? Got to go before hitting the road?"

The News looked depressed. "Why, Frank?"

My stomach lurched. "What? What do you mean, kid?" I asked. But I knew what he meant; I'd seen the look on a thousand faces over the years. The game was up. I nodded and whispered, "How did you know?"

He cocked a head toward the Port-O-Potty. "Come on, we knew Mr. Prince was high on your hate list, Frank. His colleagues told us of your blowup over the time sheets. When he retaliated by moving you up on the transfer list. . . well, we all knew how you felt about that too. Funny thing is, now you'll do more time, not less."

"Hundreds of guys hate these desk jockeys; they're always screwing up. My fight with him doesn't prove anything."

"No, but the hints you left do. You couldn't resist, could you?"

My head started reeling as he opened the door. Mr. Prince sat as I'd left him, a toilet plunger in his hand, primers on the three R's in his lap. I grunted a challenge. "Well. . . *kid*?"

"Come on, Frank. Mr. Prince, sitting on the throne with a scepter in his hand, reviewing his subjects? A child could see the symbolic resentment in the tableau you left after crushing his skull. Down with autocracy, hey? It smacks of that game Clue. Obvious, Frank."

"So I killed Colonel Mustard in the billiard room with a lead pipe? Who am I?"

He shrugged. "Mr. Green."

I saw red. "Me, envious of who, you, the rookie detective? You can't pin anything on me."

He looked so smug, and I could hear The End coming, but I'd have the last laugh. The moment I'd waited for had come; the whole scenario was coming together. I gloated, wanting to savor the moment. "For argument's sake," I said, "why go through all this if you knew?"

He shrugged. "I knew no jury would convict on what I

had, even with your prints all over the *Elements of Style*.

I must have flinched, because he said, "Oh, yeah, I lifted some good ones before finding you this morning."

I nodded. "But you knew I'd play dumb, forgetting to wear gloves handling evidence."

He shrugged. "So, I had to have you rediscover the body. You making like it wasn't there proved, of course, that you knew it was there all along."

I shook my head. "Brilliant, except for one thing." I pulled out my Glock and leveled it at his head. "Who the hell's gonna know?"

"Me."

A paralyzing pain shot through my arm and my gun fell to the ground. A huge weight propelled me against the door. It was Lido, and I suddenly remembered what had bothered me about his Rolex comment: he had used my name when I hadn't offered it.

As my hands were being cuffed, he said, "Nice work, kid, but how did you know he'd come?"

"Ego. He wanted to make sure I made the connection before killing me. The victim and the retiree, on separate and final voyages. The Port-O-Prince transfers around the city while Frank goes off to Port Au Prince, Haiti."

He answered my surprised look. "Your forwarding address was on your retirement request, Frank. You're <u>approved</u> request.

Behind his smile I read, The End.

R. J. Mills writes thriller and mystery novels from his home in Marietta, Georgia. A patented scientist, R.J. draws on his experiences as grist for the writing mill. He relies on his wife and four children to keep his feet on the ground while he pokes his head into clouds.

SWEET SMELL OF SUCCESS

The white wine was chilling; the red breathing. The caterer whipped up beef filet with truffle demi-glaze for twelve, and the florist worked his magic on the mahogany dining table. Mallory Pryor didn't have to worry about the practical details of this evening's fund-raising dinner. Her job was creating the perfect image of a Senator's wife, and she worked hard at it.

In the luxuriously renovated bathroom of the old Georgetown townhouse, Mallory blotted her lipstick on a tissue and contemplated her reflection in the gold-framed mirror. It showed the face of a woman in her mid-forties: eyes lifted by a crackerjack surgeon, skin smoothed by collagen and botox, smile embittered by life in general.

How many times had Mallory collected just the right mixture of guests—old money balanced by ambitious CEOs— and had the ambiance ruined by Jim's antics? Mallory just didn't understand it. If Jim wanted to explore a presidential bid, the junior Senator from a sparsely populated western state couldn't afford to put a foot wrong. Like every politician, he made plenty of enemies who would jump at the chance to bring him down. When they'd met, Jim Pryor had been as greedy for the top job as she was. So why did her handsome husband now seem so determined to sabotage his career?

Mallory crumpled the tissue into a tight ball and threw it against the mirror. Hot tears sprang to her eyes, but she willed them not to flow. Tonight was important, pivotal even, and everything had to be just right. She retrieved the smudged tissue, threw it in the trash and began to arrange the combs, brushes and bottles of lotions and scents on the marble-topped vanity. She made sure that her husband's aftershave stood front and center. From years on the circuit with Jim, she knew he might well find himself in their master bath with a need for a quick sprucing up.

The party started well enough. Jim greeted their guests with his practiced grin and firm handshake, then buttonholed a billionaire media mogul to discuss how the Pryor political agenda would benefit the entertainment industry. Mallory gradually began to relax. Perhaps her concern was misplaced. Perhaps Jim would behave himself for once.

Then the last couple arrived. Lars Hammond, elder Senator from Jim's home state and obligatory guest at all fundraising dinners, stepped into the living room with his latest blonde. Where had the old hound dog managed to find this one, Mallory thought, Bimbos 'R' Us?

Mallory whisked a martini off a passing tray and headed over to welcome Senator Hammond, but Jim got there first. He didn't waste a moment. Like the king of beasts stalking his prey, his blue eyes locked on the curvaceous blonde and tracked her every move. With choreographed grace, Jim passed the white-haired Senator to a seasoned contributor and hooked his hand under the girl's elbow. Mallory swallowed her fury with a gulp of vodka and vermouth as Jim unleashed his lazy, sexy smile and guided the blonde back into the hallway to admire some etchings of old Washington.

Jim Pryor was a tremendously sexual man; no one knew that better than Mallory. He'd swept her off her feet when he was new to Washington and she'd been pounding the pavement for a federal job where she could put her dime-a-dozen Bachelor of Science to work. First he'd found her a job as a chemical analyst in the Environmental Protection Agency, then he'd ditched his dumpy wife and married her. Those were the glory days—the days when Jim's sexy smile beamed for her alone and he hadn't been able to take his eyes, or hands, off her.

When had his adventurous, passionate love-making switched to automatic? When she'd been pregnant with their first? When she'd left her job at the EPA to be a full-time political wife? Mallory stretched her lips in a clown-like smile. No time to wallow in old hurts. She needed to circulate and come up with an excuse for Jim's absence.

Of course Mallory knew exactly what Jim was doing, but she doubted that their guests would open their checkbooks if they so much as guessed. Having sex in a bathroom or closet while his staff and supporters mingled right outside was her husband's idea of a great lay. Jim was addicted to risk, but Mallory refused to let his testosterone ruin their plans. She was determined to save him from himself, one way or another.

Mallory was on her third vodka martini when the blonde slunk down the hall and paused at the mirror in the foyer to make sure her skirt wasn't stuck in the back of her panty hose. Mallory smiled. It wouldn't be long now. When she had been the object of his bathroom dalliances, Jim had always sent her out first, then slapped on some aftershave to mask the scent of her perfume.

Just as dinner was announced, a high-pitched wail filled the townhouse. It was a searing scream, the sound of someone ambushed by excruciating pain. Chairs overturned. People rushed to do something, anything to help that tortured soul.

Mallory slid an olive off its toothpick with a satisfying squelch. A man with scars might not appeal to the ladies, but there was no law that the President had to have smooth cheeks. She was just glad that Jim had never taken an interest in her work. If her husband had hung around her lab at the EPA, even for a bit, he might have noticed that high quality sulfuric acid takes on a lovely blue hue not unlike his favorite aftershave.

Beverle Graves Myers writes mystery, fantasy and horror from her home in Louisville, Kentucky. Her short fiction has appeared online at Fables, Orchard Press Mysteries and Flashquake and in Futures Mysterious Anthology Magazine. Bev's first novel, INTERRUPTED ARIA, a tale of music and murder in 18th century Venice, will be published by Poisoned Pen Press in April 2004. (www.beverlegravesmyers.com)

Jeremy Yoder

BUBBLE, BUBBLE, TOIL AND TROUBLE

The only thing worse than a person dying is a celebrity dying. Not because they deserve special treatment, but because that's what they get from the press and fans—and that only makes my job harder.

Lorna McKenzie had been a teenage glamour queen in the eighties, starring in a couple dozen films before dropping out of the limelight. I recognized her name because she had been a favorite of my ex-wife, back before she had become my ex… ah, the bad ol' days.

When I received the call down at the precinct, I took a last, quick bite of my breakfast burrito, which was kind enough to drip salsa-drenched sausage onto my shirt. The morning was too warm to wear a suit coat, but I threw it on anyway to hide the stain as I'd soon be rubbing shoulders with "the elite"—and I knew they preferred Dirty Harry over Columbo.

Upon arrival, I groaned at the mob of people forming outside the mansion gates. Great. Already the story had leaked, and now I'd have to swim through the news reporters, cameramen, and nut jobs. For a moment, I had the wishful thought that my ex would be in the crowd. I could then incite them to riot and have the pleasure of spraying them with rubber bullets. Why should S.W.A.T. have all the fun?

"Sergeant Barnes?"

I looked up from my daydream to the officer's mug peering in at me. I rolled down my car window. "Sorry about that. Late night. So what's the situation?"

The fairly new recruit—I couldn't remember his name— squatted and pointed up past the gates, which exposed his nametag: Williams. There are too many Williams in the world—that's my excuse for not recalling his name… along with the sun being in my eyes.

"We only got here a few minutes ago ourselves. Forensics is already inside. We were just getting ready to clear the crowd when you pulled up. For what it's worth, some of them are asking if it's true she committed suicide. Probably just a rumor, but you have to wonder how they all found out about this so fast."

I grunted. "Maybe we'll get lucky and she's not even dead."

"Wouldn't that be nice." He looked back to the house and whistled. "Lorna McKenzie. Who'd have thought it? She wasn't even forty."

Forty. I glanced up through the windshield at the huge fence and mansion beyond. I was pushing fifty and still making house payments. "Clear me a path. Officers can come in, but no pepperonis."

He frowned. "You mean paparazzi?"

I eased off the brake and crept forward. "They're all meatheads in my book."

A few minutes later, the butler escorted me up a wide staircase, through an elaborate bedroom, and to the entrance of a master bath. Sure enough, Forensics was already there. I asked them to step out for a second so I could better survey the scene, though it didn't take rocket science to put this one together.

I stepped into a world of white marble and gold trim, which made the last five-star hotel I'd stayed at look like a Motel 6.

It was twice as big as my living room with three sinks, a four-nozzle shower room, a toilet tucked around to the left, and a large Jacuzzi along the far wall. The heat and jets had been turned off, and all the better as I can't imagine what it would have looked like if that dark, red water had been bubbling and frothing.

The starlet's head poked out of the blood-dyed water on the far side, leaning up against the back wall and staring in my direction. A row of open pill bottles and a razor blade sat along the Jacuzzi's edge. The morbid image made me think of cackling witches around a huge pot, which they'd stir with a large wooden spoon while adding all the necessary ingredients—eye of amphetamine, barbiturate of newt, and the blood of a beautiful young maiden set to simmer.

"Bubble, bubble, toil and trouble…" I muttered.

"Sir?"

I jumped and turned to see the butler beside me. Barring the body, we were the only ones in the room. His expression showed he hadn't heard me, but had instead thought I just asked a question. Thank goodness.

I looked back at her vacant expression, triggering a memory of her character in *They Only Love You Once*. In the final scene, after her seventh lover had spurned her, she ran out into the ocean in the dead of night, at which point the credits began and she slowly faded from sight. The scene always made my ex mutter, "Men," just before swatting me and bursting into tears. Now as I stared at the body, I half expected a calligraphic "The End" to appear in midair, accompanied by straining violins.

"So you discovered the body?" I said, moving toward Lorna.

"Actually, no," he replied, following. "Mr. Collins did a couple hours ago, after which he ran out of the house. A while later, he called to tell me of his discovery and that he had panicked. I found Lorna as he said and notified the authorities."

I nodded at the recollection of the out-of-work actor, Tony Collins, whom she had married a few years ago. I glanced at the butler, who stared at her with even more callousness than me. "If you'll forgive my asking, you don't seem that upset. Did you and Mrs. McKenzie not get along?"

He looked up at me with empty eyes. His paunchy stomach, droopy face, and deadpan voice made me think of a taller version of Hitchcock with hair.

"Let me assure you, Mr..."

"Barnes."

"... Barnes, that I adored Lorna. As to my lack of emotion, I've seen worse. In my previous job, I used to be a mortician."

My eyebrows shot up.

"Sorry to disappoint you," he continued, "but I did nothing to facilitate Mrs. McKenzie's demise. It is, unfortunately, just as it appears. I've already checked." With that, he rolled up a sleeve, dunked his hand into the bloody water and withdrew her arm, exposing a lacerated wrist. "As you can see, she did indeed cut herself."

"What are you doing? Don't touch that!"

My skin crawled as he placed the arm back into the water, walked to the nearest sink, and washed off. I'd seen slashed bodies handled before, but only by me and officers with rubber gloves—not average Joes off the street.

"But I can tell you this," he droned with a melted expression. "Even though Lorna took her own life, it was still murder." With that, he turned and walked out.

I stared after him, my mouth hanging open. Who was this guy? Just then, the body bag boys entered. I gave them permission to zip her up if Forensics said they were done. I then headed after the butler, now halfway down the stairs.

"Hold up one second," I said, not really expecting him to stop. When he didn't, I fell into step beside him. "What'd you mean by that crack?"

"What did you mean by yours?"

I scowled. "What're you are talking about?"

He sighed as if re-explaining something to a child. "Not only have I seen MacBeth, but I once performed the role of Banquo."

I frowned, until I recalled what I had muttered upon seeing the body; so he had heard me and just pretended not to notice.

"No need to explain," he continued. "I admit, when I first came upon the scene with the spa still running—a rather gruesome sight, if you can imagine—I had the exact same thought." He paused at the bottom of the stairs, placed a hand upon his chest, and with an air of Shakespearean drama said, "Fire burn, and cauldron bubble!"

"Uh-huh. Well, I need to ask you a few questions..."

He shrugged and resumed his walk, moving back around the staircase to a door that couldn't be seen from the front entrance. It led into a small guestroom beneath the stairs. "If you must," he muttered. Upon entering the room, he opened a closet. He withdrew a suitcase, opened it on the foot of the bed, and began filling it with various objects.

I sat in a chair near the door. "These your quarters?"

"More or less. Only a few changes of clothes. Very rarely did I spend the night."

"So where do you live?"

He sighed and paused to look at me. "I live thirty-two miles to the north. In answer to your next question, I live alone. In answer to your next question, I've worked here for almost four years. And in answer to your next question, there are two other employees that work here—a chef and a maid—that can verify anything I tell you. So with that all out of the way, please feel free to put some effort into your questioning, or you'll risk putting me to sleep."

I smiled as he resumed his packing. "All right then. What's the deal with her husband? You said he saw the body and left? Then called back later?"

"He left in a flustered rush at 9:15 without realizing I'd

seen him. At 10:35 he called, sobbing, saying that Lorna had killed herself and that he had ran out in a panic. I verified his claim and called the authorities. I then noticed a crowd gathering outside the gates." He shook his head in disgust. "Not surprisingly, he made it a point to tell those of little consequence first."

I crossed my legs. "That's a rather sensational theory, wouldn't you say?"

"As you already know, Mr. Barnes, Hollywood's all about sensationalism, and more than one career has rebounded from tragedy. There's a saying here in Tinsel Town: 'If you can't roll with the punches, move to New York so you can cry on stage.'"

"I've lived here all my life and never heard that."

"That's because I just made it up. Needs a little work, but off the cuff, rather impressive."

I forced myself not to grin. "So it's safe to say you dislike Mr. Collins."

"'Dislike' probably isn't a strong enough word. Try 'hate.'"

You had to love the guy's candor, but two could play at that game. "So let me guess. While she wasted her affections on him, you pined for her in the wings, and that's why you remained... because you were secretly in love with her."

He rolled his eyes. "I'm afraid you've seen far too many movies. This is real life—" He glanced at my graying hair. "—something I see you've been acquainted with for some time now. Again, sorry to disappoint, but I really am just the butler. If you want *Sunset Boulevard*, you'll have to rent it."

I smiled at the movie reference. "Norma Desmond. Played by..." I snapped my fingers several times, trying to recall the actress's name.

With a hard snap of his fingers, he made me look up with a start. He then deadpanned, "Gloria Swanson," before stooping to grab some shoes from the closet. "Brilliant movie. Second only to *Casablanca*. But then I am a heartless romantic."

"Yeah. So what did you mean about it being both murder and suicide?"

He paused while folding a jacket to stare off into space. For a long time he said nothing, until finally he spoke. "When a drunken husband screams at his wife that she's worthless... that she's one of life's biggest failures... that he wishes she were dead so he wouldn't have to live with her... what would you call it?"

I opened my mouth, but nothing came out. I closed it and let him continue.

"Every time he sobers up, he apologizes. This goes on for years, yet she continues to love him. Until one day she's unable to distinguish between the drunk and sober halves of her husband... or maybe she wises up and realizes there is no difference. In any case, she learns to doubt herself, and wonders if he's right." Only then did he look at me. "It'd make for quite the movie, wouldn't you say?"

I nodded as he began clearing the nightstand. "You know," I said, "in these types of situations, there are some steps that can be taken. The courts aren't entirely—"

He surprised me with a soft, brief chuckle. "Please. Neither of us is naïve enough to believe that a testimony on psychological matters of the heart would triumph over something so concrete as a self-mutilated body. And besides that, she still had her own choices to make; I can't absolve her of that." He snapped his suitcase shut and picked it up. "However, should you or someone else decide to press the issue, I'm in the phonebook. Just don't look for me here. I quit the moment I saw her body. Now if you'll excuse me, I'm late."

I frowned as he walked toward the door. "Late for what?"

"To resume my previous employment. I miss the silence."

With that, he was gone.

I leaned forward in my chair. A couple minutes later, an officer entered, asking if they could allow the butler to leave. I only then realized I hadn't asked for his name. I simply nodded, knowing I could track him down if needed. The officer then informed me that the husband had returned. I told him I'd be right there. For a moment, I told myself to press certain issues, but I already knew I'd be sticking to routine if Forensics verified it as suicide.

I exited the room and walked around to the front of the staircase, just in time to see the stretcher carrying her body descend. Nearby, an apparently distraught Mr. Collins stared up at it and broke into tears. I wondered how much of his sorrow was real and how much was just an act... or maybe I had to wise up and realize there's no difference.

Jeremy Yoder has had a handful of publications, but considers his inclusion within WHO DIED IN HERE? to be the most prestigious feather in his cap. He currently resides in Sioux Falls, South Dakota with his wife Sarah. (www.jeremyyoder.net)

James C. Wardlaw

THE CASE OF THE PORTAPOTTY HOMICIDE

"What the heck?" Jack Clark yelled to no one in particular as he jerked and yanked his fishing line back and forth
bending the pole nearly until the breaking point. "Dang, that's
either a big ole sturgeon or the biggest rubber boot in history." His line snapped flipping his pole back to the point of
hitting him square in the forehead. It raised a big welt and he
rubbed it with his fingers wincing. He looked down into the
water of Pothole Lake not sure what he expected to see, but
what he did see was a bluish green thing that looked like a
long box as it resettled toward the bottom of the shallow lake.

He threw his boat anchor in to see if he could snag it with
something larger than twelve pound test fish line and after
several tries, he had snagged the thing. He started pulling,
but it was too heavy to get it very far and he had to let go just
as it neared the surface. But what he did succeed in doing
was identifying the green box as a portable outhouse. He
saw the moon shaped window cut into the side and the vent
tube sticking out the top like a huge soda straw before it sunk
back into the darkness and slime at the lake bottom.

The thing wasn't really important to Jack, except that it
represented a challenge and he never shied away from a chal-

lenge until he'd either succeeded in conquering it or failed so miserably that he would be depressed for a week afterward. So, he pulled it just off the bottom and tied the anchor rope to the back of his boat.

The twenty-five horse Johnson started on the first pull of the starter rope and he clicked it into forward and forged ahead. The boat squatted down at the stern, but made headway dragging the Portapotty slowly toward the shore. When he could go no further, he jumped out of the boat and proceeded to roll the box over and over out of the water and up onto the beach. As it breached the surface, water poured out the two windows.

As he rolled the thing, there was a clunking sound from inside kind of like the sound a pair of tennis shoes makes in the dryer at home. He imagined all sorts of things it could be from a huge large mouth bass to a bag full of drug money hidden by some unhappy drug dealer. Either one would have been cool in Jack's opinion.

By the time he'd gotten it about three-quarters out of the lake, he couldn't wait any longer and as soon as the door was on top, he pulled on the handle. Nothing! "Blast it!" He shouted and pulled harder. It still wouldn't budge. He went over to his boat and opened his toolbox. Inside was a pry bar. Taking the bar, he broke open the outhouse door and then flipped it back. He fell backward as he saw what was inside rolling around. It was the body of a woman. He sat down with a bump in the wet gravel and just stared at the opening, then cautiously stood back up and peaked over the rim of the opening.

There she was, muddy blond hair looking like so much fine seaweed in tangles over her face. What skin he could see near her neck and the upper part of her breasts was bluish green and soggy looking. Her formerly white blouse was streaked mud brown and her skirt and panties were wrapped around one leg, presumably falling off the rest of the way while he rolled her over and over in the box. He imagined her sitting on the seat, minding her own business, when wham, she was knocked into the lake somehow. He figured she'd drowned unable to get out. But, *how the heck did she get so far out in the lake?* He wondered as he stared at her lower body. His mind strayed to something more morbid and sick than he wanted to admit and he shook his head like a rattle to clear it from those thoughts. *I better call the cops.*

Jack waited near his boat for nearly an hour until the Sheriff's white blazer roared down the dirt road and skidded to a halt, just inches away from the outhouse lying on its side. Two uniformed officers jumped out and came around to inspect the scene. Jack told them the story and they poked around the woman's body with gloved hands being careful not to move her very much until the coroner arrived. They did put her legs together recovering a little modesty for her sake. It did not look like a rape.

Before long, the coroner's hummer pulled up and a man and a woman in lab coats got out both with large cases. They opened them and one took a few pictures while the other one made notes and then moved the woman's head, arms, and legs, presumably checking for signs of foul play.

Jack peaked over the open door to see that she had been very attractive, looking to be in her twenties. The examiner was just moving a hunk of matted hair.

"She was hit on the head, but it doesn't look like it was what killed her." He said as he twisted his head up to look at the woman with the camera. He moved and she took a few more close-ups. "We'll have to open her up to see if there is water in her lungs, but I am guessing that she drowned." He opened her mouth with his pen and looked inside. He started to let it close when he did a double take. "Hey, there's something in her mouth, here. Give me the long forceps."

She handed him a pair of huge tweezers and he used them to reach down her throat to grab something. Jack could see that he was having difficulty pulling out what was lodged in her throat. Finally, he pulled out a large gold fish.

"Stupid carp!" He said as he turned it over and around with the forceps. "Maybe she didn't drown after all."

She had started to stink, as she lay there exposed to the hot sun and Jack and the two deputies held their noses. The coroner's people seemed not to notice the putrid odor. "Hey, guys, how about giving us a hand getting the lady on the stretcher and into our truck?" The female examiner said.

Jack could see the script sewn into her lab coat. It said Jennifer Crosley, MD. He couldn't see the man's name as a pocket protector full of pens and a short ruler covered the embroidery.

After the coroner's wagon had left, the deputies dusted for prints and left, thanking Jack for reporting to them.

Jack sat there on the side of his boat for a few more minutes, thinking about the once beautiful woman and wondered what her story was. *I probably won't ever know.* He thought as he got up, pushed the boat out into the lake, started the motor and cruised off back toward the launch ramp. He'd had enough fishing for the day and maybe for the rest of his life.

Drs. Crosley and Tompkins performed the autopsy on the woman that evening, discovering that she had choked on the fish and had minimal water in her lungs. It appeared that she had been rendered unconscious, thrown in the outhouse and then the whole thing had been tipped into the lake. They doubted that the fish had been crammed down her throat, but that it had wandered into the outhouse as she was coming to and got caught in her throat in her attempt to breathe. The head wound had been made by a cylindrical object with some sort of plaque attached to it. The plaque had a crest or coat of arms of some kind carved into it and that pattern had been embossed into the woman's scalp.

Her prints matched those of a local college student, Carrie Kendal. No one realized she was missing as she often left her apartment and stayed out for days. Her roommate told the deputies that he'd last seen her on Tuesday, three days before.

"I think she had been seeing one of her teachers, but I'm not sure which." Tom her roommate said.

"Did she have any other man friends?" Deputy Jardeen asked. "You know, that she might have been with in the last couple of days."

"I don't know. I only found out about the teacher from her girlfriend, Katie, I think is her name in 23D down stairs. She and I had a little, well...never mind."

Deputies Jardeen and Conley thanked the fellow and went down stairs to visit Katie in 23D.

"Yeah, she was playing around with Professor Garret. She told me that she had the hots for him and they did something about it two weeks ago." Katie confessed. "I think that they were doing it like a couple rabbits, lucky girl. So what's the big deal? She show up dead or something?" She laughed.

"As a matter of fact, she did." Conley said.

Katie's face turned ashen like that of a corpse. "Holy s...! What happened? You don't think Garret did it, do you?"

"We don't know who did it at this time." Jardeen answered. "But we're going to go talk to him after we leave here."

They left Katie sitting on the couch looking like a cyborg with its power cut off, blank eyes staring into nowhere and little tears just beginning to overflow her eyelids.

"So, Professor, we hear you have been somewhat indiscreet with one of your students?" Jardeen said as he sat down in the chair Garret waved him to. Conley wandered the office looking at the books on the bookshelves lining the walls. He kept his ears trained on the conversation without appearing that he cared.

"I could get in trouble for that." Garret answered. "Or is this the trouble?"

"No, not that kind of trouble, but one of a much worse kind, Professor." Jardeen answered. "We found Carrie Kendal dead out at the lake. Any idea how she got that way?"

Garret kind of fell back in his chair and nearly tipped over backwards as his face turned the same color of ash as Katie's did. "How did it happen?"

"She was hit over the head, thrown in an outhouse out at the lake and tipped into the water to drown. They even pulled her skirt down to make it look like she was going to the restroom and just sort of fell in the lake. Any idea who would want her dead?"

Conley's cell phone rang and he picked it up. "Yeah, OK." He flipped it closed, went over to Jardeen and bent down to his ear. "The prints on the outhouse door weren't in the system so it's a bust so far."

Jardeen nodded and turned his attention back to Garret.

"No I don't. She was just a student, not into anything, just going to school and, well, doing it with me." He looked uncomfortable. "I think my wife suspected something, so I broke it off three days ago. Carrie didn't seem too heartbroken. It was just a fun thing. We didn't get too heavy. I don't think she expected me to leave my wife for her or anything."

"By the way, where was your wife three days ago?"

"I have no idea. I guess she was at home. I don't keep track of her comings and goings; why don't you ask her."

The deputies left and drove over to the Garret's house to talk to Tammie Garret. She invited the officers in and had them sit down. Jardeen couldn't understand why Garret would look elsewhere when his wife was so beautiful. He wanted her himself and started to imagine him with her in the kitchen when Conley spoke up.

"Mrs. Garret…"

"Call me Tammie, deputy." She cooed in a sultry voice that made Jardeen return to his fantasy.

"Mrs. Garret, where were you three days ago?"

"Why deputy…" She paused to look at Conley's nametag.

"…Conley?"

"We're investigating the murder of a young woman. She was a student at the college."

"Why ever would you ask me that? I don't have much to do with the college unless Davis has to go to some function and takes me along."

"Just tell us where you were. Mrs. Garret."

This time Jardeen acted like the disinterested party and got up to wander the study, looking at the knick-knacks, dust catchers, as he liked to call them.

"Well, I don't rightly remember, but I think I went to the garden club for lunch then over to the florist to pick up some flowers for the dining room table, then to the grocery to get some steaks for supper. Yes, that's about it, I suppose. Then I came home to fix supper and wait for Davis to get home from work." She glanced across the room as Jardeen sauntered over toward an étagère full of what looked like fraternity mementos.

As he neared it, she got up and walked over to him. He was just starting to pick up one of three long pewter beer mugs with the fraternity crest embossed in the side.

She grabbed from him the one he picked up and placed it back on the shelf. "Those are Davis' and he doesn't really like anyone to pick them up." She smiled as if it was difficult to do so and it came over her face looking forced and fake.

"Where is the fourth mug, Mrs. Garret?" Jardeen asked.

"I have no idea, deputy. Maybe Davis lost it or broke it. I don't keep track of his things."

"Well, thank you so much for your time, Mrs. Garrett." Jardeen said. "We'll probably get back to you later."

They drove out to the lake and searched around the area where the outhouse had once stood. They were about to leave when… "Hey, Jardeen, come here." Conley called. "Look what I found." He held a tarnished pewter fraternity mug hanging from his ink pen.

Jardeen pulled out a ziplock and Conley dropped the mug

into it and sealed it up. Let's get this in for prints, but I think I know whose we'll find." Conley said as they got in the car and left.

"Mrs Garrett, you have the right to remain silent...."

James C. Wardlaw has been writing for over 20 years and has written and published over 250 articles and short stories and three books. He resides in Tennessee. (www.jamescwardlaw.com)

SHELTER IN THE SHADOWS

"Everything will be all right." Ivy heard her mother's soothing voice in her head as she peered through the slats of the closet door at Lyle and Barbara. Her fiancé and best friend worked into a sexual frenzy while she watched from her blind. Her plan to surprise them backfired, and now she found solace within the dark closet as the sexually spent couple cuddled.

"I love you," Lyle said, and slid from the bed to retrieve something. "Will you marry me?"

Ivy froze. *Marry?*

The redhead forced the ring over her knuckle. "Oh, Lyle! Yes!" She admired the ring. "Can we afford it?"

"Yeah, we're set. Frank will think Ivy took the money. I paid Dan half, he's in."

"Ivy won't know what hit her," Barbie said. "She's dumber than a doorknob."

Ivy buried her rage with years of expertise.

Lyle glanced at his watch. "Look at the time!" He hurried into the bathroom across from the closet.

Ivy shifted her position. *Pop, pop.* She watched Barbie's blood spatter across the bed and onto the wall.

"What the hell is goin' on out here?" Lyle asked from the bathroom door. *Pop.* The force of another bullet threw him into the tub; the shower rinsed the rush of blood from his shoulder. *Pop. Pop.* His lifeless form filled the tub while his existence spiraled down the drain.

Ivy gasped for breath and pressed against the rain soaked brick. The stench of garbage strewn in the alley triggered her gag reflex, as silhouettes of three men stopped to look into the dead-end. She held her breath; listened and squeezed her eyes shut praying they would disappear; their voices muffled by the falling rain.

"Spread out," one man shouted, sending one of the three toward her. The petite blonde scraped her back along the mortar and allowed the shadows to swallow her. She crouched into a doorway and onto the ground in a fetal position. Her gloved hand pushed plastered hair from her eyes as she gently rocked back and forth.

Ivy watched as Danny Bard maneuvered the dank passageway. She willed herself to stop rocking when he paused nearby. "Ivy," he called, as if he could be trusted. She didn't move. After an eternity, he turned and exited the dead end. She blinked at her reality, the alley, her ruined dress, and blood on her gloves. The doorway offered shelter, and the young woman allowed exhaustion to thrust her into a fitful slumber.

Sergeant Glenn Boyd carried coffee in one hand while he lifted the yellow crime tape with the other. He eased his large frame under the tape and hurried past squad cars parked outside the motel. Their lights accented the steady rain and cast slashes of color across the numbered doors.

"What's up?" he asked two uniformed officers standing under the overhang. Glenn glanced at the seven painted on the opened door.

"Two bodies," the freckle-faced cop said. "Shot. What a mess." He shook his head.

Glenn sipped his coffee. "Guess seven wasn't their lucky number," he said and walked into the cramped room. "What ya got, Carla?" he asked the woman wearing latex gloves.

She finished dusting the headboard for prints. "The lady in the office heard gunshots and called 911 around 8:15," she said as she stretched her back. "Those two cops outside found 'em, called us, and secured the scene."

"We have one male, white, thirty-five to forty years old, shot three times." Her thumb indicated the bathroom where the flash of a camera bounced off the mirror. "Here," she nodded toward the bed, "female, white, twenty to twenty-five years old. She took two." He walked over to the bed, lifted the bloody sheet, and let it fall.

"Our witness saw a late model, cream color Lincoln leave the scene."

"Weapon?" he asked, and swallowed the last bit of cold coffee.

"Probably a .357 Magnum." She displayed a collection of spent cartridges. "One more thing, we found this empty jewelry box."

Boyd studied the evidence. "A ring?"

"Yeah, looks like someone ripped it from her finger," she said. "We haven't found it."

"I. D.?" Boyd asked. He walked toward the bathroom and peered at the carnage.

"Lyle Goodman," she said. "The girl...Barbara Cook."

"I need a cigarette," he announced, and walked out. He huddled beneath the overhang, watched lightening rip the sky, and searched for his lighter. The best thing he could do for forensics was stay out of their way.

"So whad'ya think?" the freckle-faced cop asked and offered a light.

Boyd lit up. "They knew the perp," he said as thunder rolled in the distance.

A heavy-set woman looked up as Boyd entered the office. "Miss Bard?" he asked.

"Ms.," she corrected.

"Detective Boyd," he introduced with a flash of his badge. "What can you tell me?"

"I already told the cops," she complained. "I heard shots, and saw a Lincoln peel outta' here. Almost hit the truck painting that center line out there." She pointed. "Just one thing."

"What's that?" he asked.

"What happened to the blonde I let into the room?"

"Blonde?" He collected pertinent details. The blonde was a regular, as were the victims. He stepped outside, lit up another cigarette, and returned to the scene.

"We have a possible lead," Carla called from inside.

Glenn took a deep drag and threw his half-smoked butt into a puddle. "What is it?" he asked leaning against the doorjamb.

"Barbara Cook worked at the Pleasure Palace."

"I know the place." In his soul he wished to be home in a warm bed next to a loving wife. Right now he'd settle for the warm bed.

The vacant streets made for a quick trip to the Palace. As Boyd pulled into the parking lot a half dozen cars dotted the storefront. "What do we have here?" he asked himself. He reported the Lincoln parked next to the one story building and sent for backup. Last year the owner of this joint was charged with racketeering, but got off on a technicality. It left a bad taste in Glenn's mouth.

Boyd stepped from his car into the drizzle using his flashlight to examine the Lincoln. Nothing out of the ordinary caught his attention until the beam exposed a patch of yellow on the rear tire. He reported his findings and went inside to talk with the owner of the car.

Muted bump and grind music seeped through the empty teller's window. Boyd checked for a buzzer. Posters of the Palace's featured dancers decorated the wall. His eyes focused on large red letters, "Barbie Doll." Barbara Cook stood in her black, thigh-high boots while she yanked the pigtail of a young blonde, sporting the schoolgirl look. The blonde's handle, "Ivy League."

"Twenty bucks, plus two drink minimum," an older voice crackled through the intercom in the middle of the window.

Boyd held his badge up to the glass. "I'd like to talk with the owner."

The woman sipped her drink. "He's busy."

"He won't be busy if I shut the place down."

"Is that a threat?" the old broad asked.

"No. It's a fact," he said pushing his badge into his pocket. "I'd suggest you comply."

"All right, don't get your panties in a bunch." She picked up the phone. "There's a cop here. Wants to see Frank."

One of DiLena's goons ushered Boyd through the smoky room, past the half-nude dancer pleasuring the pole and down the hall to Frank's office. "Sergeant Boyd." DiLena stood in mock respect. "We meet again." He gestured toward a chair opposite his desk.

Boyd chose to stand. "I'll cut to the chase. Where were you tonight around 8:15?"

"Here," he said palms up.

"Can that be corroborated?"

"Why?" he asked coldly.

"Two bodies and a cream color Lincoln leaving the scene," he said, patting his pockets for his cigarettes.

Frank's demeanor changed.

Glenn lit up. "One of your dancers."

Frank straightened. "Ivy? I haven't seen her since my driver dropped her at the motel down the road."

"Real name, Barbara Cook?" Glenn asked blowing smoke into the air.

"Barbie?" Frank asked.

Boyd nodded. "What's your driver's name?" he asked.

"Daniel Bard, why?"

The detective's cell phone interrupted. "Boyd...I see...Thanks." He clicked the phone off.

"I'm taking you in for questioning. You can come along on your own volition or we can make this messy."

"I don't know what you're trying to pull," he protested.

Boyd read him his rights and slapped cuffs on his wrists.

Back at the station Boyd held DiLena as a suspect, but organized a surveillance team to watch the loose ends.

The following afternoon, Frank, clad in his orange jump suit, eyed the detective suspiciously. "I want my lawyer," he complained.

"Our search warrant turned up the murder weapon in your car. You willing to talk off the record?"

"What's in it for me?" DiLena slouched into the chair.

Boyd's dislike for this guy wrenched his gut. "I believe you're innocent."

Frank straightened. "Yeah, right."

"Get this," Glenn leaned across the table, "I don't like you, but it don't add up. Tell me what happened. The paint on your tires puts you at the motel, and the murder weapon found in your car—it's too neat."

"I didn't do it," Frank emphasized. "Okay." He held up his hands in surrender.

"Off the record?"

Boyd nodded.

"I have money missing…a large sum." He guarded his words. "Ivy called upset, said Llye had the money at the motel. I went to the room. The money wasn't there…they were already dead. I swear to God I didn't do it."

"Can I talk to this—Ivy?"

"I told you, I haven't seen her. Her and Frank were supposed to get married. She might've gone home."

Glenn pulled into the long drive to the old farmhouse. Valarie Pernell, alias Ivy League, occupied the swing on the porch.

"Miss Pernell?" he asked as he shuffled up the stairs.

"Yes?"

The youthful woman looked even younger than her school-girl image. "Sergeant Glenn Boyd, Mecklenburg Homicide Division."

"Out of your jurisdiction, aren't you?" she asked.

"I'm here out of curiosity," he admitted.

"Have a seat," she invited. She looked at him with wide, innocent eyes.

"Thanks," he gestured for her to stay seated.

"What can I do for you?" She tilted her head.

He cleared his throat. "You left Mecklenburg kind of sudden." He watched for a reaction. "I wondered why."

She hesitated.

"Frank's in jail," he said. "For murder."

"Murder?" She covered her mouth. "Frank?" she asked. "Who?"

"Barbara Cook and Lyle Goodman, can you help?"

Valarie picked at her thumbnail and nodded. "Barbie and I were friends," she admitted. "Lyle was my fiancé. He talked me into a three-way." She looked away, as Glenn watched a blush color her cheeks. "I didn't want to do it. They asked me to hide in the room and pretend to catch them and join in. I said no, but changed my mind. I didn't want to be left out. When I arrived, the lady in the office let me in, and I hid in the closet."

"The closet?"

She nodded. "The timing never felt right to surprise them, so I stayed in the closet. I saw them murdered," she confessed.

Glenn shifted forward in his chair. "What do you remember?" he asked, digging for details.

"I couldn't see the killer." She shrugged. "They thought that money would change their lives, and now they're dead, and the killer has the money."

"What money?" Glenn pretended ignorance.

"Frank kept stacks of money in his safe," she explained as she chewed her bottom lip. "Lyle took the money. When I told Frank about it, he flew into a rage."

"Frank saw you after the murders?" Boyd asked.

"No, I called him. Told him I wasn't coming back." Her big eyes blinked. "I can't believe Lyle is gone." Her voice quivered. "I'm afraid. They tried to pin the blame on me for the missing money."

"Are you here alone?" he asked.

She nodded. "Daddy disappeared shortly after mom died." The petite blonde stared into the distance at nothing. "Too many memories for him to live here," she explained, as her mind drifted to another time and place while she nervously turned the diamond on her finger. She blinked and her attention returned to Glenn. "It's part of life," she said with a shrug.

The detective found the statement odd. He sensed emotional baggage.

"I'll make sure you're safe," he promised. "You want to pack some things?"

"Okay." She disappeared into the house. Glenn walked to his car, called the local authorities and checked on the surveillance team back in Mecklenburg. When he returned to the porch he heard a faint voice. He followed it to the outhouse behind the house. There, he peered through a knothole to see Valarie talking to thin air.

"I'm going away, Daddy." She kissed her soiled glove and dropped it down the hole. "You told me city men were no good. You were right. They're like you," she laughed uncontrollably. "Lyle got what he deserved, just like you," she seethed.

Glenn waited outside the ramshackle structure, and escorted the blonde to the back seat of his car, where they waited for the local authorities.

"New charges of racketeering were filed against Frank

this morning," Glenn said over lunch, a week later.

Carla sat across the table salting her fries. "They tied the money to him?"

"Yeah, who'd ever guess it?"

"So how do you know Ivy didn't do it?"

"The gun," he said as if that explained it.

"And?" She waved him on with a fry.

"She had access to the weapon, but Dan Bard dropped her at the motel and left."

"Ivy couldn't have planted it back in the car," Carla realized. "What about Frank? I'm surprised you didn't let him cook."

"He's scum, not a murderer."

"Once I learned the hotel clerk's son worked for Frank, I put surveillance on him. Bard's prints were all over the gun. Daniel Bard and his mother recognized Ivy's mental instability and figured she'd take the rap. When she didn't return to the club it threw a wrench into their get-rich-quick plans. They claim they're innocent, but they have the money, or should I say what's left of it. Guess they couldn't wait to spend it."

"What about Ivy?"

"Institutionalized," he said sadly. "Her father messed her up real good." He took another bite of his burger. "The authorities found traces of human DNA in that outhouse, but nothing conclusive."

Valarie rested against the padded wall of her dim, closet-like cell. She heard her mother's soothing voice. "Everything will be all right." She closed her eyes and dreamed of the satisfaction of squeezing the trigger and spending her money.

———————————

Donna Sundblad resides in Florida with her husband Rick. Her published credits include a course developed for Writer's Village University, and short stories published at Writer's Hood, and Night Wind the Fiction Magazine.

Sandra Levy Ceren

SUMMER HOLIDAY

Meg pushed open the door of the women's restroom in the lobby of the posh Plaza Hotel. The door closed softly behind her. "Oh my gosh, this is the most beautiful loo I've ever seen."

"It sure is," Ellen said, following behind her. Meg was inspecting the décor while Ellen hurriedly opened the door of a stall. "Oh, no!" she screamed. "Call 911.

There's a dead woman on the can."

The women ran out into the corridor. Meg called the police from her cell phone.

Ellen started to run back into the restroom. Meg yelled after her. "Don't go in there. The police said we shouldn't touch anything and to wait right here for them. They'll call hotel security to meet us and prevent anyone from entering the Women's room."

Ellen's face turned stark white. "But I'm going to vomit."

" Use the Men's," Meg said, pointing to the room opposite from where they were huddled. "I'll stand watch outside."

Meg stood guard. She could hear the gross sounds emanating from her friend inside.

When Ellen came out, she was flushed and her face was moist. "I feel a bit better, but I don't know if I'll ever be able to use a public restroom, again."

A tall, bald, sturdily built dark man in a pin stripped suit hurried toward them. "I'm Hal Black from hotel security. Are you the people who reported a problem to the police?"

"Problem? It was a real trauma. I never saw a dead person before, and in such an unexpected place."

"How do you know she was dead?" Black asked.

"Her eyes were wide open, but they didn't blink. There was blood all over her legs, like she'd hemorrhaged to death. I'll never forget it. Her limbs hung loosely like a rag doll."

"Did you see a knife, or a gun shot wound?"

"No. Maybe she died from natural causes. A real shame. She was so young."

"How old might she have been?" Black asked.

"She appeared to be my age, mid-twenties. I don't know. Maybe younger. Could even be late teens. Very pretty. Natural blonde hair, light blue eyes. Looked like one of the many Russian immigrants we've seen around here. "

"How do you know she was a natural blonde, Ellen?" Meg asked.

"She wasn't wearing panties."

Meg blushed.

A police siren grew louder and louder as the car came to a stop outside the hotel. About a minute later, two uniformed officers appeared. They took statements from Meg and Ellen and copied down their identification information.

As Meg and Ellen walked through the lobby, two paramedics carrying a gurney hurried in the direction of the restrooms.

"Let's get away from the hotel," Meg said. "Go somewhere for tea. It may soothe your stomach."

"Good idea," Ellen answered.

They stepped out of the hotel. It was a sunny summer day, but they were shivering. Meg checked her watch. "I think the Russian Tea Room serves all day. Let's walk over."

Arm in arm they walked a short distance to the ornate

café. The interior was decorated with a huge brass samovar and colorful Russian artifacts. They ordered a pot of tea for two.

"What a way to spend our hard earned summer holidays," Ellen said.

"Well, we chose New York because we wanted romance and adventure."

"Instead, we find ourselves in the midst of a horrid situation. At first it seemed we were going to be hauled into police headquarters as suspects. Those cops were very suspicious."

"They're trained to be suspicious, Ellen. Every unusual death must be investigated as a potential homicide. A young woman found on the commode of a posh Manhattan hotel restroom warrants investigation. If we'd murdered her, we'd need a motive. We don't know her. We have no connection to her. And why would we call the police and wait around for them? We're two harmless Midwest teachers on holiday in the Big Apple."

"Yes, but the police need suspects and may frame innocent people," Ellen said.

"Detectives will be assigned to the case. Probably there are crime scene techs at the hotel right now looking for clues." Meg tried to pacify her friend.

"Yes. And my fingerprints are all over the door of the stall," Ellen cried.

Meg leaned across the table, her chin in her hand. "Yours and many other women's. It's a very popular hotel restroom. It's bad enough for you that you had to find her, but now you are making it worse by worrying that you'll be suspected. Maybe she died elsewhere and was dumped on the can quite recently. How it was done without detection is curious."

"You're right, Meg. I'm worrying needlessly. I just can't get it out of my mind."

The server deposited a colorful ceramic teapot at their table. "Will there be anything else?"

"Perhaps later." Meg smiled.

Ellen poured the tea. "Let's see," she said, over the rim of her teacup. "If she died elsewhere and then was dumped in the restroom, how and when could someone have carried her in there without being seen?"

"How big was she?" Meg asked.

"She was petite, slim. Maybe ninety pounds. I couldn't tell her height from her position, but I'd say she was short."

"So, it is possible a strong person could have placed her inside one of those hanging, canvas carrying bags that no one would notice in a hotel lobby," Meg offered. The murderer or accomplice could have walked into the restroom unnoticed, entered the stall, dumped the body and walked out with an empty bag. It'd be easy to get rid of the bag in a big city with all its garbage."

"Good thinking Meg. The bag could have been dumped in the restroom. I don't recall seeing it, but I was a bit distracted," she chuckled. "I remember from my mystery book reading group, there must be method, motive and opportunity. So let's work on possible motives."

"Big cities have drugs and prostitution problems. Maybe she was a run-away kid who hooked up with the wrong people. Maybe she was about to report a crime. The bad guy found out her intention and had to stop her so he murdered her."

"A likely possibility, Ellen. Maybe she was the child of two warring parents and one killed her to hurt the other."

Ellen rolled her eyes. "That's just awful, Meg. You've got quite an imagination."

The server returned to the table. "May I bring you anything?"

"Is it okay if we just sit here a little while longer?" Meg asked.

"Well, we're not busy, yet. We have some delicious Babka. It's Russian coffee cake, a specialty of the house. It has chocolate and cinnamon."

Meg and Ellen looked at each other and smiled. "Sure,"

Ellen said. "We'll share a slice."

The waiter frowned and walked away.

"Big cities, eh?" Ellen said.

The entry door opened and two pale, blond men of indeterminate age walked in and were taken to a nearby table.

Meg and Ellen immediately changed the subject and began to plan the rest of their vacation. They would attend a concert at Carnegie Hall, a film festival at Lincoln Center, and take a docent tour of the Metropolitan Museum.

They couldn't help overhearing the men's loud conversation conducted in Russian. It was obvious the men couldn't have known that the two American women within earshot were Russian teachers.

The two men addressed each other as Sergei and Igor. Meg whispered, "Prokofiev and Stravinsky."

From the men's conversation, they learned that Sergei's sister had botched another abortion and couldn't be trusted to do another, since this time, the abortion had resulted in the death of young Larisa. Not to worry, Sergei's sister had gotten rid of the body at the Plaza hotel and no one in America would miss Larisa.

Meg and Ellen stifled their gasps.

The server placed a large slice of Babka on Meg and Ellen's table. He brought a bottle of vodka and two glasses to the men.

"Excuse me, Ellen. I'll be back in a minute." Meg slipped her purse strap over her shoulder and went outside to phone the police.

Sandra Levy Ceren, a native New Yorker, is a psychologist in Del Mar, California. A popular newspaper columnist, she is frequently interviewed on TV and in the press. Her short stories have been published worldwide. PRESCRIPTION FOR TERROR, her first novel in a series introduced psychologist - amateur sleuth, Dr. Cory Cohen. SECRETS FROM THE COUCH is the second in the series. (www.DrSandraLevyCeren.com)

Lori G. Armstrong

PRAYING TO THE PORCELAIN GOD

The squeak of a key turning in the lock echoed through the quiet room, yet she remained motionless.

She knew the drill by now. Wait, stay silent, and pray.

Still, she didn't stop the quick shudder of anticipation when the door opened and his footsteps shuffled across the tile. In the pristine silence the tiny sound became deafening. No white noise was allowed. Nothing registered in the cavernous house but the unsteady clamoring of her heart. She realized if he heard that rapid fire *lub-dub*, *lub-dub*, he'd punish her. He expected peace and quiet. A gentleman, he claimed, rarely raised his voice.

He wasn't a gentle man.

Eyes downcast, she leveled her breathing. And waited.

He inspected her first, before ridding himself of the stench of the piety of the world in which he worked with gallons of hot, purifying water.

He crept across the carpet with the stealth of a jungle cat seeking prey, lingering behind her, batting at her hair. Sometimes he examined her nails for minute specks of dirt. Upon declaring her filthy, he then scrubbed her fingers until the cuticles turned bloody. If her scalp appeared unclean, he'd dunk her head in the stool.

Tonight he took his time. But she knew he couldn't find fault. Everything was perfect; *she* was finally perfect, even when he'd told her repeatedly, in his patronizing, dulcet tone, she'd never been the woman he'd wanted.

Tonight that would change.

His fetid breath drifted across the nape of her neck, damp, sticky as a dirty sponge. She lowered her eyes as he began to slowly circle the table, searching for proof of her insubordination. When he clapped his hands loudly next to her ear, she didn't flinch.

Did her obedience please him?

No. It never did.

He slid into the captain's chair across from her, the marble between gleamed black as his mood.

The table had been scrubbed to a high sheen as was required. He insisted cleanliness was next to godliness.

He wasn't a god.

"Audra," he murmured on an exigent sigh.

Don't look up, don't look up, she whispered the mantra inside her own head, fearful even her private thoughts were thunderous. But the pull to seek his approval was too strongly ingrained. She glanced up and met his dark, taciturn stare.

First, he said quiet disapproval with his eyes. Then with his fists.

Yes. She knew the drill. Wait. Stay silent. Pray.

Except tonight, she refused to pray.

The first incident happened on their one month anniversary. A little wine, a little song, and she'd accidentally charred his steak. She'd actually laughed.

Then punch drunk had taken on a whole new meaning.

After she'd vomited in the bathroom, he'd become enraged in that eerie, hushed manner, taunting her; even praying to the porcelain god wouldn't save her from punishment.

The penalty had to fit the crime, he'd admonished, forcing her to scrub the toilet blindfolded with undiluted bleach until her fingers had cracked, her flesh peeled nearly to the bone. He believed himself to be a dispenser of justice.

He wasn't a fair man.

Yet, he'd never marred her face, blackened her eyes, or broken her nose. He made certain to hide his marks of possession where only he could admire them. Swollen patches of flesh where he'd pinched until her fair skin protruded in ugly bumps, the red slap of his hand prints on her stomach and buttocks, the crusted skin where his nails scored her until she'd bled, remained out of sight-out of mind. The neat rows of bite marks were worse in the winter, hidden under heavy layers of clothing. He'd been particularly proud of his Valentine's Day gift: a ring of sorts—a ring of purplish black bruises resembling tribal tattoos which circled her upper arms. They lasted two full weeks, much longer than a dozen red roses.

She knew she wasn't to blame, but she hadn't bothered to tell another soul. Who'd believe her? He was beloved, a gentle man, a quiet man, a godly man, a fair man. At first she'd been his equal, a woman reared in a respectable church-going family. With no history of spousal abuse, she didn't fit the societal mold, a young, broken girl so desperate for love and attention she'd gotten sucked into a familiar, familial cycle. No, she'd been unlucky enough to start a new cycle all her own.

But tonight that cycle would end.

The promise of summer hung outside her sparkling windows, short skirts, short sleeves, short tempers.

She fondled the gun perched on her lap. No silencer. Giddy, loud laughter burst forth on the inside. She envisioned red splatters on the spotless white shower curtain before his blood swirled down the drain. Afterwards, she wouldn't bother cleaning up.

Praying to any god, porcelain or otherwise, wouldn't help him.

No. Tonight he'd be the man *she'd* wanted all these years; not a quiet man, not a gentle man, not a godly man, not a fair

man.
   A dead man.

Lori Armstrong lives in Rapid City, SD with her husband and three daughters. She is currently working on the second mystery of a series set in the beautiful Black Hills.

A. S. Berman

SILENCE

Closing his eyes against the sunlight seeping into the tiny bathroom, Detective Harriman imagined himself sitting instead behind the wheel of that sporty little cabin cruiser he'd hit the river with someday soon, if only the weather, and his pension, held out.

Kneeling down beside the kid, Harriman finally opened his eyes. Taking in the red-flecked walls and shower tiles, he couldn't help thinking it was all there somewhere–the ebb and flow of life–glistening at him. Bits of January last, perhaps, congealing across the off-white drywall, or maybe recollections of a midnight stroll with a significant other whose significance had since faded with time.

In all, a lifetime of someone else's memories surrounded him, brought to the surface with a single squeeze of the trigger. And for the first time in a long while, it bothered Harriman that he could not recognize each trickle of blood for the memories they contained.

"For heaven's sake, Jack," Ruth sighed, plucking the cookie from her husband's hand with an irritated groan as she returned to the stove. "You're going to spoil your appetite."

Harriman thought about the blood-soaked toilet across

town. The eyeglasses neatly folded on the coffee table just outside. The instinctive way they all slanted the barrel right up to where the peanut butter sticks to ensure a speedy end, and the annoying habit the hard palette had of slowing that bullet every damn time.

"Spoil my appetite," he mumbled absently. In the other room, the television set mused to itself, "On the road of life, there are passengers and there are drivers."

Six days the kid laid there on his little patch of yuppie Shangri-la, wedged between the sink and the bloody commode. He'd probably have been there still had the couple below not returned early from an Australian excursion to find their new carpet ruined, a victim of a badly hemorrhaging ceiling from days before.

Ruth followed him into the dining room with a tray of bread rolls, swaying a little to the jazzy intro of the celebrity-gossip show that now replaced the car commercial, until the ringing phone broke her mood.

"Every time," she grumbled. "Every single time. It's getting so you can't even hear yourself *think* anymore."

She wasn't always like this... Harriman told himself, muting the TV before picking up the phone.

"Hello? Hello?" he called over the crackling connection, a legacy from the lightning storm they'd weathered two nights back.

Faint murmurs of other conversations rose and fell over the line until his boss' blustery "Damn it, hello" emerged from the static.

The cop lost no time prodding Harriman on the status of the Jeremy Banks suicide report.

"Know you've got a pretty heavy caseload, but if you can just knock this one out quick, it'll get headquarters off my back."

"Headquarters?"

"Parents want to get this all behind them — you know how it is. They're starting to lean on us to wrap it up. Too unseemly…who knows."

Silence.

"You *do* think it was suicide…"

Harriman sighed. "Suicide, yeah."

He promised the report would be finished by the end of the week.

No sooner had he hung up than Ruth swept into the room to crank up the volume on the TV.

"…took us behind the scenes for an exclusive look at his new movie…"

Harriman sank his teeth into a roll, watched his wife flutter around the kitchen a bit, and tried to remember what it was he'd been thinking about before the phone rang.

Stepping into the cordoned-off apartment at No. 23 Cherry Hill Court was, for Harriman, remarkably like tumbling back into a bad dream only recently escaped by the seat of one's pajamas.

"What are we looking for, exactly?" With a sniff of boredom, Detective Blumfeld gave the bathroom a good once-over for anything that might've been missed by the clean-up crew.

"Not sure," Harriman admitted, fighting to be heard over the whine of an industrial-strength carpet cleaner coming from the apartment below.

Blumfeld glanced back at his partner peering dreamily through the living room window.

"Jack?"

Harriman shook his head, staring out over the empty parking lot. "Kid sits down, takes them glasses off, gobs a pistol barrel and … bang!"

Blumfeld shrugged uncomfortably. "Happens, I guess."

"A .38 goes off in a building – in the most echo-prone room in an apartment – and no one hears?"

"It was suicide, Jack."

"I know," Harriman sighed, glancing around the small

living room, catching his distorted image in the dead gray glass of the TV set. "It was the loudest sound this poor slob could make, and in the end, no one heard a thing."

Closing the door of his study against the sitcom laugh track down the hall, Harriman returned to the folder he'd been poring over most of the night.

Paper-clipped to the inside, a faded snapshot showed three young men and a pair of women, arms slung over each other's shoulders as they mugged for the camera, Jeremy Banks among them.

Jeremy Banks. Twenty-five. Investment banker on his way up the career ladder. Fifty grand a year and his own parking space ...

Click.

Two weeks of vacation time ...

Bang.

Silence.

The following night, hours after he'd put his signature to the Banks report, Harriman got in his car, cranked the stereo up until he could feel the bass thumping in his chest, and drove.

Not until the familiar towers of Crestwood Station peeked over the horizon did he realize where he was headed.

Coasting into the gated community behind a line of returning residents, the cop tried to remember which of the cookie-cutter apartment houses had been the kid's.

He shuddered.

In the soft glow of the streetlights, Harriman found in the open buildings a transient quality that bothered him more and more each time he saw them.

Each apartment opened out, motel-fashion, onto a common airy walkway. All that seemed to be missing was the gurgling of the ice machine by the stairs.

Rounded arches framing the building entrances brought

to mind lonely small town train stations – an architectural nod to the subway depot just down the road, he supposed.

Flapping at him in the evening breeze, a neon yellow flyer tacked above a row of steel mailboxes declared, *Come join us for a Fourth of July blowout! Enjoy refreshments and conversation before the fireworks in the Crestwood Station clubhouse.*

Fireworks.

Before leaving the office, he'd cornered his boss with the question he kept coming back to again and again.

"Have you ever heard a .38 go off?"

"Jack –"

"Don't say it, all right. I know it was suicide. But damn it, no one in the building knew that at the time!"

Somewhere on a higher floor, a door slammed and a young couple galloped down the stairs without giving Harriman a second look.

The detective moved down the hallway, hovering a moment at the first door on his right, the familiar chimes of a *Jeopardy* contestant's mettle being tested interrupted only by the call and response of muffled voices inside the flat.

Across the hall, a baby cried over a bass-studded pop tune, a woman's irritated shouts adding a strange descant to the fractured melody.

On he walked.

Canned laughter. Jazz beats. News reader monotones. From behind each door drifted a different soundtrack, as different as the smells that wafted out to him on the evening breeze.

Finally, he came to the last door on the right.

Silence.

Letting himself in with a key he should've returned days ago, Harriman was surprised to find every light in the place burning.

Alone in the place for the first time, Harriman now noticed how sparsely furnished it was. One maroon sofa, one glass coffee table, one bookcase.

And a conspicuous absence of those items the detective had long equated with the lifestyles of the upwardly mobile. No stereo. No speakers. No CD cases stacked high on dusty shelves.

How much had the kid scrimped to afford his little place on the "right side" of the tracks? Just what had it cost him?

Moving through the living room, he caught his dour-faced twin staring back at him from the dark glass of the television set.

Before Harriman even hit the "on" button, he knew what he would find.

Silence.

Only a tiny, multihued dot deigned to appear, floating mockingly at the center of the screen.

All around him, the residents of Crestwood Station were safely cocooned by the din of their television sets, their stereos – the soundtracks of their lives. Had Harriman chosen that moment to squeeze off a few rounds from his own service pistol, he knew no one would have heard it.

Never before had he realized just how heavy silence could weigh upon a person, nor how loud his own thoughts could echo when, after a lifetime of countless distractions, he was finally forced to listen to himself think.

"Hello? Hello Jack, is that you?" Ruth called over the crackling line. "It's almost 10 o'clock. Where are you?"

As if in reply, a pair of distant voices emerged from the static.

"Damn this phone," Ruth muttered.

It was great seeing you today, said the first voice, a young boy's.

Oh, you too, said the girl. *I had so much fun. Maybe next week –*

Starting to call Jack's name again, Ruth stopped, smiling

instead at the familiarity of the phantom conversation taking place in the background.

The girl said, *I'll see you in class tomorrow*, waiting a moment before adding, *Aren't you going to hang up*?

You first, the boy insisted with an adolescent tenderness that nearly broke Ruth's heart. Hadn't she had the same exchange with Jack a thousand times when they first started dating so many years ago?

"Oh Jack, please come home," she whispered into the phone before the phantom voices receded into the static.

Phone tucked under an ear, Harriman peered out through Jeremy Banks' window at the small satellite dishes on the neighboring porches, each craning a blank round face up to the heavens, as if awaiting divine inspiration.

You hang up first.

No, you.

Harriman smiled. How happy they'd been in those days. But that was then.

Come on, one of us has to hang up first.

Gently, Harriman lay the phone down in its cradle.

Tomorrow he would leave her, he knew that now. And there, alone for the first time in their quiet house, Ruth would finally be able to hear herself think.

A.S. Berman has written for USA TODAY, the Gannett News Service and other national publications. He lives in Maryland with his wife, Susannah, and is the first to admit that he knows more about 'Buffy the Vampire Slayer' than anyone probably should.

PROBLEM PLUMBING

"Mommy, I have to go," Stevie said as he tugged on his mother's pants.

"Uh huh, dear. Just a minute." Molly flipped through the Pete's Plumbing Palace folder of bathroom fixtures trying to decide what to do with her remodeling project. "Should I go antique or modern?" she asked herself.

"Mommmmie," he whined and pulled harder.

"One minute, Stevie, and I'll be done." She pulled the fabric and paint swatches from her purse and laid them next to the antique faucet.

Her friend Sergio, who worked at the hair salon next door, had volunteered to come with her. "I'll keep you safe from Pelvic Pete," he said, but she wanted to do this herself. He threatened to stop by if his schedule allowed, but she firmly refused. Just because he was gay didn't mean that he had the best taste in home decorating. She'd seen his apartment, she knew.

Even her husband, Bill, offered his assistance, but she said, "You're just like Sergio. First, you confuse me with your suggestions, and then I end up with what you want, and it's not even close to what I wanted in the first place."

She walked to bathroom display with a modern design. Her red paint and black samples clashed with the futuristic angles. "The other one looked better, right Stevie?"

But she heard no reply.

"Stevie?" She looked around the bathroom display, but no one was there. She wandered back to the antique display. No Stevie. He knew better than to hide from her, and he would never go off with a stranger…

"STEVIE!" Her voice rose to the shrill that she hated… "STEVIE!" She ran from one display to the next, shouting his name.

A blonde clerk with a severe haircut rounded the corner in the maze of bathrooms. "Ma'am, can I help you?" Her tone said, "Keep it down," and her body language spoke of anything but help. Her dark eyes darted nervously around the displays as she tapped her toe on the floor. She glanced at her watch and said, "We'll be closing soon."

"I…" Molly started to answer, when Stevie emerged from a bathroom display to her right.

He adjusted the zipper on his pants. "I'm right here, Mommy." His happy voice was unaware of his mother's panic.

Molly rushed forward and hugged him, forgetting about the clerk. "Don't you ever do that to Mommy again," she said.

"Do you need anything else," the clerk's monotone asked, "Ma'am?"

"No," she answered.

The angular woman looked Molly up one side and down the other before she turned on her heel and walked away.

"Where did you go?" Molly asked. Then she smelled it. She breathed in deeply. "Stevie? Did you have an accident?"

"No, Mommy," he shook his three-year old head.

"But I smell…"

"I did it all by myself, Mommy." A huge smile crossed his mouth.

Molly's heart stopped. "What did you do all by your-self?" But she was afraid she knew.

"I'll show you." He grabbed her hand and led her to a display bathroom in the back corner. He walked over to the stool and lifted the lid. "See?"

Molly tentatively stepped forward.

"I did number one and number two," he beamed.

For the last year, Molly and her husband had been trying to potty train Stevie. Bill had him housebroken. Stevie would pee off the back deck, but he hadn't figured out how to use the toilet by himself.

"But Stevie, there's no water in the toilet." *He couldn't have.*

"I pulled the handle, but no flush."

"Oh no," Molly stopped as she looked into the bowl. *He did.*

"What did you do?" she said between her clenched teeth. Then she remembered all the work they had done so far to get him to do just this. "What a good boy! What a good boy." *What the heck am I going to do now?*

Stevie's brow wrinkled. His mother was upset and he didn't know why.

What can I do? What can I do? Molly looked around frantically. *How could he have known it wasn't plumbed? How would he know that it was only a demo, not a usable toilet? What do I do?* A huge smile played across her lips. *He used the bathroom for the first time!*

Then the image of the unfriendly clerk came back to Molly's mind. *There is no way I'm going to tell her what had just happened.*

"What's wrong, Mommy?"

"We need to think, Honey." *What am I going to do?* She bit her lower lip. Her eyes scanned the room and glanced into the next display. A hand towel hung from a bar next to a pedestal sink. Molly raced forward and grabbed it. She ripped it off the bar, ran to the toilet, and threw the cloth inside. A clicking of heels approached, and a shadow suddenly appeared.

The evil clerk was back. "Can I help you?" Her eyes narrowed on Molly.

Molly slammed the lid down and turned around. "Just checking out the waterworks."

The woman sniffed the air and frowned. "Do you smell that?" Her eyes bore into Stevie.

He and Molly shook their heads.

"Well, let me know if you need any help," but her tone barked, "hurry up and leave." She looked at her watch again and walked back to the front of the store.

Suddenly, Molly's cell phone rang. She reached in and pulled it out. "Hello?"

"Hi, Hon, how's it going?" Bill's voice asked.

"Don't ask."

"Has Pelvic Pete made a pass at you yet?"

Molly didn't answer.

"Okay. Sorry to joke about that. Sergio and I did offer to go with you, remember?"

Silence.

He took a deep breath and exhaled. "Did you decide which…"

"I can't talk right now," Molly said breathlessly into the phone. She pressed the red button and threw the phone into her purse. She lifted the lid of the stool and peered inside.

The yellow fluid was absorbed into the towel. She looked down at the folder in her hand. She reached into the bowl and picked up the towel by one dry corner, at least she hoped it was dry. She flipped the damp towel into the folder and slammed the toilet's lid down.

Molly sat down on the commode and gently placed the folder on the floor. The clerk appeared one more time and stared at Molly. The clerk tapped her foot a few times on the floor and walked away.

Molly waited a few seconds and opened the toilet. It was still there.

"Mommy, I'm hungry."

"Just a minute…" and then she stopped. *Asking him to wait was what got me into this mess in the first place.* "Stevie, Mommy needs to clean this up first, and then we can go find Daddy." *And when I find Daddy I will tell him how well his idea worked to take you along…* "I need another towel," she said out loud to herself.

Stevie pointed to a white towel draped over the shower curtain rod.

I can't use a white towel! She told herself.

"We need a different one, dear." Her tone was calm and soothing outside while her inner yelled, *What are you thinking? Like the color of the towel is going to matter at this point anyway. It's not like you're going to use it again.*

"You need a different what?" the female clerk's voice demanded.

Molly spun around. "I need a different color for my bathroom at home."

"But Mommy, you said…"

Molly's hand shot out and covered her son's mouth.

"Maybe you should check out the displays in the front of the store. They seem to be more to your … liking. And everything up there is on clearance. We'll be closing soon, so tomorrow…"

Clearance? Did she look second-class? Molly looked at her reflection in the full-length mirror. Her black hair was spiked by Sergio to perfection, just like his own blond hair. A black leather jacket covered her red "Go to Hell I'm Reading" T-shirt. Okay, so she didn't have a bra on, but it's not like she really needed one. Hot neon pink spandex legs stuck out of her cut-off denim shorts. Black leather boots rode to mid-calf. Same thing she wore to work at the used bookstore. *What was wrong with this get-up?* Molly's anger was rising. *Was it this woman or was it me?*

"I'll be done, when I'm done," Molly said. She saw a black towel in the display to the left.

It wasn't what the clerk wanted to hear. The clerk clinched

her fists. Her arm muscles tensed under her sweat stained, but otherwise tightly pressed suit. She glanced at her elegant wristwatch and tapped the crystal. When Molly didn't respond, she walked briskly away.

"What is her problem?" Molly asked as she snatched the black towel. She stormed over to the stool, lifted the lid, dropped the towel in, and grabbed it.

"It's just like picking up after a dog, it's just like picking up…"

Molly removed her hand and wrapped the towel up. She slammed the seat down and stuck the second towel into the folder. She repositioned the folder and held out her other hand to Stevie.

"Come on, Honey. Let's get out of here." Molly held folder so the towels wouldn't show or leak.

She pulled Stevie along through a few more displays, before she found the public restroom. Molly pushed the door wide open. As they rushed into the room, both stopped in their tracks. "Oops!" Molly said. "Sorry, I didn't mean to…" and then she realized what she was seeing.

A man sat on the toilet with his pants down around his ankles. At first sight, he looked like he was sleeping, but his pale, blue skin and slightly protruding tongue told a different story.

"What's wrong Mommy?" Stevie asked.

"Nothing!" exploded from her mouth. *Act natural. Don't scare Stevie. Don't panic!*

Molly shielded Stevie's eyes and turned his little body the other way. As she turned to follow him out of the room, she read the name badge on the man's shirt. "Pete" was stitched in red thread.

"So, have you had enough of Pete's Plumbing Palace? What a butch place this is. I prefer Homo Depo, but that's just me." Sergio appeared in the doorway, blocking their exit. He rolled his eyes. "I had a few minutes between clients and thought I'd just pop over next door and see…" He sniffed the air and wrinkled his nose. "God. Who died...?"

Molly's mouth fell open. She tried to wave him back, but Sergio stepped into the room and waved his hand in front of his nose.

"I know you wanted to do this all by yourself...oh excuse me, sir," he said as he noticed Pete. Then he did a double take. "Oh my God! Is he...?"

Molly nodded.

Sergio pointed to Stevie. "Does he...know?"

Molly shook her head.

"Okay, then." He took a deep breath and stepped back. "Did you want to come over to the salon? I really need to show you something, NOW!"

Molly swallowed hard and pushed Stevie forward. "Let's go. I can't wait to see what you have to show us."

Sergio took one more look at Pete. "You'd think his plumbing would be bigger."

"What?" Molly stopped in her tracks and gave Sergio a look that told him he was way out of line.

"This place looks so much bigger on the outside than on the inside." And then he got it. "Oh, you thought I was referring to..." He turned to point at Pete and stopped.

But he didn't get to finish. The female clerk suddenly appeared with a gun in her hand. "Stay right where you are."

All three held their breath.

"I tried to get you to leave, but no. I told you we were closing, but no, you took your own sweet time."

"Just let us go. We won't tell anyone." Molly pulled Stevie to her side, pushing him between her and Sergio.

"Like I believe that," the clerk said.

"It's not like anyone is going to miss Pelvic Pete, right?" Sergio asked. "The stories I've heard over at the salon would curl your hair."

"I'm sure they were all true." The clerk shifted her weight to her other leg as her gaze turned to him, but she said nothing.

"You did this town a favor," Sergio added.

"Why did you kill him?" Molly demanded. She pressed Stevie into Sergio.

"Kill Pete?" the clerk asked.

Molly looked out of the corner of her eye, hoping to catch Sergio's.

One of his hands lowered and touched Stevie on the shoulder.

Molly nodded at him and pressed Stevie into him again.

"I didn't kill him. It was an accident," the clerk said. "I could only take so much of his groping and sexist comments." She took a deep breath. "He called me into the storage room. I thought it was for a problem with inventory, but as soon as I walked in, he grabbed my breast, and the next thing I knew, I was hitting him over the head with an acrylic plunger."

She swallowed hard. "He complained about having a bad headache and that he was going to throw-up, so he went to the restroom." She pointed the gun in his direction. "That's how I found him. I must have hit him too hard."

Molly pressed Stevie against Sergio, hoping he'd understand, when she almost dropped the folder, but she tightened her grasp as it slipped. Once it was firmly held, she immediately hid it behind her back.

"What do you have there?" the clerk demanded, as she saw Molly's arm movement.

"Nothing," Molly said, quickly. She pushed Stevie into Sergio and extended her other hand further behind.

"What are you holding?" The gun waved in circles as she advanced.

"You don't want to know."

"Yes, I do."

"Molly, what are you doing?" Sergio asked from between tight lips. "Give it to her," he said with his hands in the air.

"No," is all Molly said.

The look of unbelievable shock stood out on his face. Molly could see that Sergio didn't understand why she was refusing to listen to this person waving a gun in her face.

The clerk took another step forward. She pointed the gun at Molly and spread her legs wide to brace herself.

At the same moment, Sergio grabbed Molly's purse and Stevie. He shielded Stevie's body with his own as they rounded the corner of the next display.

Molly's arm came out from behind her back and she pitched the folder and towels at the clerk. The folder opened and the wet, soiled towels flew through the air.

The clerk raised her gun arm to fend off the objects. Molly ran forward and tackled the clerk at the waist. Her body slammed into the woman and forced her to fall back. The gun arm flung backward and hit the floor as the gun fired.

Molly pounced onto the clerk's chest, reached across her body, and pinned the woman's arm to the floor. Her nails dug into the clerk's wrist and slammed it onto the ground. "How dare you point a gun at my son!" she yelled. She continued slamming the clerk's hand onto the floor, despite the woman's gagging and choking. The hand struck the tile and suddenly the weapon flew out of her grasp.

As the gun skidded across the floor, Molly pulled her arm back and hit the woman square in the face. She pounced and kneeled onto the clerk's arms and sat down hard on the woman's chest, pinning her to the floor.

Sergio dialed 911 and it was only minutes until sirens and flashing lights filled the store windows. Two officers burst through the door. Searching the store, they found Molly in the back sitting on the clerk. "Freeze!" They shouted at the same time.

Molly released the woman and held her hands up.

One of the officers stepped closer. "Slowly," he warned.

Sergio's head popped up from around the corner with a toilet tank lid in his hands and the cell phone at his ear. "She's not the one. That's the one who pulled a gun on us," he said pointing to the clerk with the porcelain.

Stevie's head popped up next to Sergio's holding a toilet

scrub brush. "Yeah," he said shaking it at them.

After a few strained minutes and a lot of convincing from Sergio, the police explored the public restroom and discovered Pete's body. All the pieces fell into place, and the officers finally understood what had really happened.

"I thought she was being rude, asking me either leave or look at the clearance items in the front of the store. Do I look like I need to buy at a discount?"

Before anyone could answer, she continued. "I thought she just wanted to close the shop early. I didn't know she killed her boss and wanted us to move away from the back of the store. All she would have had to do was ask..." Molly stopped talking.

"We know, Ma'am."

"Sergio, give me my phone." Molly took it and hit a few buttons. "I need to call my husband."

The officers were handcuffing the clerk and walking her out of the store when Bill arrived.

Stevie ran to his father and hugged him tightly. "That lady was mean to Mommy, but Mommy showed her. Mommy tackled her."

"Really?" Bill asked as he lifted Stevie into his arms. "What else did I miss?"

Molly took a deep breath, but Stevie added, "Daddy, I used the potty all by myself!"

"Great job, Champ! I always knew you could do it."

Sergio and Molly burst into laughter. "Come on. Let's get out of here. Do we have a story to tell."

Lance Zarimba has published two short stories: "Reservations for Home" in the Vermillion Literary Project (winner of the 2001 VLP short story contest) and "The Case of the Boogered Books" in the Mayhem in the Midlands anthology. Lance is an occupational therapist in Sioux Falls, SD working on a "Therapy" mystery series.

DARK REUNION

Laurie arrived at the reunion alone. Her husband David begged off, saying he wouldn't go to his own reunion. "Those things can dredge up adolescent garbage," he said. Later, his words would come back to haunt her.

It was an hour's flight from Halifax to Saint John. She took a cab from her mother's and now she wasn't sure why she had come. She never was part of the "in-crowd." Still, she found herself looking forward to seeing a few of the people again.

The gym was bright, noisy and festive with balloons in the school's colors of red and blue. She scanned the crowd for a familiar face and spotted Harold Thomas across the room. He was doing a smooth move to Barry Manilow's *Mandy*. Laurie smiled. Harold didn't look any different, just older.

She turned to see a woman in a purple pantsuit rushing toward her, smiling hugely, "My God, Laurie Stevens. You look the same as you did in high school." She held her at arm's length. "You have no idea who I am, do you?"

"Well, I..." Laurie paused.

"Can't blame you. I've put on a few pounds. I'm..."

"Alice Moore," Laurie jumped in, grateful to have remembered. "It's great to see you again," she said, meaning it. "How are you?"

"Not so bad. The name's Dowling now. Divorced," she added with a shrug.

Both women turned as a male voice greeted them. Laurie recognized the sexy, boyish grin at once. She'd had a crush on Aaron Hamilton, while all he could see was the blond and popular, Jillian Thorne. He was still tall and good-looking, but his thick sandy hair was a thing of the past. Other people joined them, and at some point they all gravitated toward the buffet table and, in particular, the generously laced punch bowl.

Laurie noticed Jillian Thorne heading in their direction, looking like something out of *Vogue* in a yellow strapless number, her handsome doctor husband in tow. The local paper did a big spread when she married the heart surgeon. Laurie thought he looked uncomfortable, perhaps like David would have looked if he had come.

Within minutes Jillian grabbed center stage, just like in the old days. She touched Aaron's arm while she talked animatedly. Laurie felt herself go quiet inside, as always whenever Jillian was anywhere near her. *You're a grown woman with two grown children,* she reminded herself. It didn't help. David was right. There was something slightly masochistic about school reunions. *I'll give it an hour. Then I'm out of here.*

"Hello, Laurie."

Laurie turned to see a stunning woman in a caramel silk suit-dress, the skirt coming nearly to her ankles, the shirt loose and flowing, smiling tentatively at her. Straight auburn hair ending just below her ears gleamed like satin under the lights. "Elegant" was the word that came to mind. Laurie stared hard, but nothing clicked. "I'm sorry, I ..."

The woman smiled and put out a hand. "You always were so nice. Always caring of other people's feelings."

Laurie sensed something familiar about the woman. Her eyes were beautiful, as clear as crystal pools.

"You probably don't remember me. I'm Margaret Dross."

Laurie was stunned. "Margaret, of course I remember you. You look fabulous. What are you doing now? Are you married?" *My God, I can't believe this woman is the same girl who sat at the back of the room, with stringy hair and glasses and tiny eyes that were practically lost in mounds of extra flesh.* Margaret had been painfully shy with a fanatically religious mother who would rant at her, usually within everyone's hearing.

"No," Margaret said. "I still live with my mother. She's not well. I'm a bookkeeper but I have my own office. A cubbyhole, actually, but I like it."

"You always were a whiz at math."

"I like the way I can make things come out even in the end," she smiled.

Laurie remembered Margaret walking along the school corridor, shoulders hunched forward, shoelaces clicking on the polished floor.

A peal of laughter drifted from the buffet table.

"I can use a little more punch, Margaret. How about you?" She touched a hand to the woman's shoulder.

Margaret drew back. "No, you go ahead. I'll just walk around a little." She smiled again as she moved away. "You look really pretty, Laurie. That color of blue matches your eyes."

Laurie understood Margaret's reluctance to go into the lion's den. School couldn't have been much fun for Margaret. She was always alone. Sometimes Laurie would seek her out and share a sandwich with her. *Why is she here, if not to show off how great she looks?* Laurie wondered. *Damn, I really want Jillian to see her. I want Jillian's husband to see her. Nasty, Laurie. Nasty.*

When Laurie returned to the table to refill her glass, the good doctor was apologizing for having to rush off, leaving Jillian with a half smile on her face. Laurie thought he looked relieved, and wondered if he arranged to be called away.

You have such a devious mind, Laurie Stevens Dobson.

Laurie didn't see Margaret again until she was leaving. A few taxis were lined up in front of the building. Margaret caught up with her as she was going down the wide cement steps.

" Laurie, can I give you a ride?"

"Well, if it's on your way..."

"It doesn't matter. I don't have anywhere to go. Are you staying with your mom while you're here? Is she still on Visart?"

"I'm surprised you remem..."

"I remember a lot, Laurie. It's that blue station-wagon right there." She unlocked and opened the door. "Hop in."

"Thanks, Margaret," Laurie said, sliding into the passenger seat. "This is sweet of you and it'll give us a chance to get caught up."

"You have two boys," Margaret said, surprising Laurie again. "Your husband's into computers." She switched on the ignition. "I never did find Mr. Right. What with the job and taking care of Mom there hasn't been time for socializing."

"Oh," Laurie said, nodding, wondering why they were sitting with the motor running. Suddenly she felt something hard press into her ribs and looked down, thinking it the buckle of an errant seatbelt. She only felt bewilderment when she saw the gun in Margaret's hand. She thought it might be some sort of weird "reunion" joke, until she looked into Margaret's eyes. "Margaret, what are...?"

"Just be calm, Laurie. It's not you I want to hurt. You were always nice to me but I didn't know how else to get Jillian into the car. Her husband's departure like was a stroke of luck. There she is now, just coming out of the building. Call her, Laurie. Tell her we'll give her a ride."

"Margaret, this is crazy..."

The gun jabbed her ribs, making her wince. "Call her before she gets into that taxi or you'll be sorry."

Say no, Jillian. Be the snooty bitch you always were and say no. Past the tightness in her throat, Laurie called out to

Jillian through the car window. But Jillian didn't say no. In fact, after peering in the window she smiled her cheerleader smile and hopped into the back seat.

"Thanks. Hey, it's still early, ladies. Why don't we all go for a drink? I know a terrific jazz club."

Jillian obviously had had one too many. "That sounds like a fun idea, doesn't it?"

Margaret shot her a look. Laurie remained silent.

"Laurie said your name was Margaret?" Jillian leaned over the front seat to closer scrutinize her driver. "I can't remember any Margaret in our class except for..." She let out a small chuckle and Laurie's stomach sank. "But that's obviously not you, dear."

The car bolted forward, nearly striking the taxi in front. Margaret didn't slow down until they were halfway up Main Street, then she made a sharp right, pulling into an alley. She turned in her seat and pointed the gun on Jillian.

"Get in the passenger seat, Jillian. Laurie, you drive. I'll get in the back."

"What is this? A joke? " Jillian asked, indignantly. Before she could say another word Margaret struck her with the gun. At the sickening crack, Laurie instinctively made a grab for the weapon. In the next instant she was staring down the barrel.

"Don't be stupid, Laurie."

"Okay," Laurie whispered, drawing back. She glanced behind her to see Jillian sitting with her hand pressed against her cheek, weeping softly.

"Who are you?" Jillian asked.

"I'm getting out now," Margaret said, with a deadly softness. "Jillian, you get in the passenger seat like I told you."

The alley was so narrow there was barely room for them to squeeze through the doors, but at last they were all in their assigned places. Jillian still clutched her face but stopped crying. The clock on the dash said 10:55 p.m. Laurie told her mom she would call if she would be home later then eleven.

She told her mom there was a chance she could end up having a really good time. *Right.*

Five minutes later they were turning into a paved drive on Douglas Avenue. Laurie knew it was a white, Victorian-style, fronted by a high cedar hedge, ancient elms, like sentinels, on either side. She'd passed it many times on her way to the museum, though she never knew that Margaret lived here.

Margaret ushered them into the foyer. Even before she switched on the light, Laurie could smell the oppressive mustiness of the house. The smell of Vick's was in the air. And something else - something dark, deeper, that Laurie couldn't discern.

Limp, yellowing doilies covered the backs and arms of overstuffed furniture. A dusty piano stood against the far wall. The rug Laurie stood on was Oriental, its design barely visible. A grandfather clock stood in the corner beneath the staircase, its pendulum still.

Margaret asked for their coats, as pleasantly as if this were a social call and she was the welcoming hostess. *She's mad*, Laurie thought, *stark, raving mad.*

Margaret led them, at gunpoint, through a small hallway into the kitchen. She shoved Jillian into a hard-back chair near an old-fashioned wood-burning stove. She handed Laurie a length of white cord from the table in front of the window. A green window blind shut out the world.

"Tie her up."

Laurie saw the narrow back door was bolted shut. She wondered how long it would take her to release the bolt and run. Laurie looked at the dishes piled in a chipped enamel sink. She inhaled deeply. The place stunk.

"My mother was a lazy, demanding woman," Margaret said, as if reading Laurie's thoughts. "She made me do all the housework. I've become quite slovenly myself. I hate this house." Margaret grabbed the cord from Laurie's hands and gave it a hard yank that made Jillian cry out. "I said tight, Laurie. Use a little elbow grease, as my dear Momma would say."

With a silent apology, and averting her eyes from Jillian's, Laurie drew the rope taut around the pale, thin wrists.

"Good. Now wind the cord around those two back middle rungs, and double knot it. Then, do her ankles."

Jillian looked terrified. *You're not the only one*, Laurie thought.

As Laurie was making the final knot, Margaret stepped forward and grabbed a handful of Jillian's hair and snapped her head back. " How does it feel to find yourself at someone else's mercy? But you have no mercy, do you?"

"Please, I have money. My husband will..." Jillian pleaded.

"Shut up!"

I have to do something, Laurie thought. If there was to be an opportunity for escape, she knew she would have to create it, although she had to be careful. Margaret's attention was on Jillian but she also kept a wary eye on Laurie.

This is a nightmare, isn't it? I'll wake up any second, Laurie thought.

Laurie steeled herself. "Margaret, I have to go to the bathroom. All that punch, you know..."

Margaret waved the gun in the direction of the living room. "Upstairs, second door on the left."

Laurie mumbled a "thanks" and went through the hallway with tentative steps, half thinking that it was a trick and that any second a bullet would slam into her back. The front door seemed a mile away, as if she were looking at it through the wrong end of a telescope. She wasn't sure if Margaret had locked it. If she could open it, she wouldn't stop running until she'd alerted the police. She edged towards the door.

"I'll kill her the minute you close the door after you, Laurie," Margaret called out, calmly. For one shameful instant Laurie asked herself what Jillian had ever done for her? Then she turned and resignedly went up the stairs.

Laurie quickly checked the two bedrooms on the right. The second room smelled strongly of Vick's and faintly of rosewater. An open Bible lay on the night table. Beside it was a phone. With her heart racing, Laurie eased the receiver from its cradle and put it to her ear. There was a kind of "whooshing" sound, like the sound heard when listening to the inside of a seashell. Laurie pressed the button trying to get a dial tone.

Suddenly, the "whooshing" was replaced by the terrifying sound of Margaret's voice. "Hang up, Laurie."

"Margaret. I was just calling my mom. She'll be worried..."

"Hang up. Now. You disappoint me, Laurie. I thought you understood." The phone clicked off.

A claw foot tub dominated the bathroom. A plastic curtain was drawn across it. Laurie sat down on the toilet, listening to the slow drip of water into the tub, something - something, made her reach out and draw the curtain back slowly, as if in some part of her mind she already knew what she would find.

The woman's splayed feet were revealed first. They were swollen, with dark bluish toenails that badly needed cutting. Her mottled flesh was as white as bread dough. Laurie did not remember her being such a large woman. Mrs. Dross would not have fit in Laurie's small apartment-sized tub. Pale eyes stared up at her from beneath a skim of water and her mouth was slightly open. Tendrils of wispy gray hair floated about her face.

Laurie closed the curtain and fought to keep from passing out while bile rose bitterly in her throat. She had to get hold of herself.

Oh, my God, Margaret murdered her mother.

Laurie returned to the kitchen. She looked closely at Jillian, still tied to the chair. She could see the scars at the corner of her eyes from Jillian's eyelift. Jillian's tears had washed away her makeup.

I have to do something.

"Could we have tea?" Laurie asked, forcing a smile.

"You've been terribly hurt, Margaret. We should talk about it."

"Talking won't make the nightmares go away. You don't know what she did to me, Laurie."

"I think I do."

"She took pictures of me in the gym shower and showed them around the school."

Laurie had a vague recollection of the incident.

"They all laughed at me. The boys said ugly, horrible things to me. I told my mother, but she said I probably deserved it. She said it was punishment from God. So, no tea, Laurie. There won't be time."

"I didn't mean any harm, Margaret," Jillian said in a small voice. " It was just for fun. We were kids."

Please, please let this work, Laurie thought.

"Fun for you," Laurie yelled at Jillian. "Your laughs were always at someone else's expense. You need to understand what you did. You need to atone."

Jillian twisted in the chair. "Why are you ganging up with Margaret?"

"Why not? You always had your gang," Laurie answered as she glanced at the owl clock on the wall.

Mom will be looking for me by now.

Margaret looked at Jillian and lowered the gun a little. "I've always wanted to ask you why. Why me, Jillian? Why were you so cruel? What did I ever do to make you hate me so much?"

" I didn't hate you."

Laurie knew that was probably true. Margaret had meant nothing to Jillian. She was as insignificant as a fly on the windowsill, except as a target of amusement.

"Do you remember daring Jason Belding to ask me to the school dance, Jillian?"

"No," Jillian whispered.

"I thought he liked me. I spent all my baby-sitting money on a new dress. When I got to the dance, he was with one of your friends. You had this smirk on your face. You made him to do it. Everyone wanted to please you, Jillian. You had it all."

"You're wrong, Margaret," Jillian said. "You..."

"Do you remember you and your friends following me?" Margaret went on. "Chanting 'here pig here pig, oink, oink'," Margaret said, hunching over and crossing the floor and back, as she mimicked the ugly scene that would never leave her.

Jillian closed her eyes. Laurie knew she remembered as well as she did. Laurie tried to make them stop, but they wouldn't. She could still hear the stomp of feet following behind Margaret, marking time with the hateful chant. They didn't even stop when Margaret stumbled on the sidewalk, crying as she searched for her glasses. Laurie was the one who helped her up and found her glasses. Jillian and her pals had gone off, laughing.

"It was twenty years ago, for God's sake," Jillian said, to Laurie's utter amazement "You should be over it by now."

"Over it?" Margaret said quietly.

Jillian strained against the ropes. "Do it then," she cried. "Just go ahead and get it over with. Will it make you feel better to know my life is crap? My 15-year old daughter ran away. My husband is divorcing me. And I'm well on my way to being an alcoholic. So if you want to kill me, Margaret, do it. You'd be doing me a favor."

Margaret looked as confused as Laurie felt. It was hard to think of Jillian Thorne's life as anything but perfect.

"Let her live, Margaret. You'll be punishing her more. You don't want to hurt anyone. Give me the gun."

"She was all I had and she's gone," Margaret cried out.

Laurie realized Margaret was talking about her mother. "What happened to your mom, Margaret? What made you...?"

Suprised, Margaret said, "I would never hurt my mother, Laurie, I loved her. She had a heart attack."

It hadn't occurred to Laurie that Margaret's mother had died of natural causes. Relieved, she said, "We should call an ambulance."

"Isn't it a little late for that? See, I might as well be dead too," Margaret said, looking at Jillian. "And so should Jillian. It's because of her that I have no one."

"Margaret, it's true you were a victim of childish cruelty, but it's over."

" Margaret, I'm sorry, " Jillian said. "I didn't know..."

"Sure you did." Margaret said, lifting the gun for the last time.

It's now or never.

Not daring to give it further thought Laurie dove at Margaret. The gun flew out of Margaret's hand and slid across the linoleum floor under the table. Laurie rolled off of Margaret and scrambled after it. Margaret's hand clamped around Laurie's ankle, but it was too late.

Flinging herself on her back, Laurie gripped the gun with both hands, aimed it squarely at Margaret.

Margaret's eyes filled with tears. "I thought you were my friend."

"I am," Laurie said. "Believe me, I am."

It was after two in the morning when Laurie arrived back at her mother's. "You really must have had a great time," her mother said, busying her self with teapot and cups, despite the hour. "Tell me everything."

Laurie smelled freshly baked chocolate chip cookies. Her favorite. There but for the grace of God — and Mom.

"You wouldn't believe it, Mom. You just wouldn't believe it."

Joan Hall Hovey enjoys, as well as penning suspense novels, short stories and articles, narrating books and scripts in her home recording studio. She lives in Gondola Point, New Brunswick, Canada, and is currently working on her next novel. *Dark Reunion* is condensed from the original short story published in *Investigating Women: Female Detectives by Canadian Writers* (Simon & Pierre, 1995). (www.joanhallhovey.com)

Dean Johnson

SENT FROM UP ABOVE

Through the zoom lens of his 35mm Nikon, from his seat in a tree house high on a hill above the Huntsman's Inn, the Colonel watched a little black speck moving along the road that led from the highway. The little black speck grew into a large red Cadillac with a "Just Married" sign mounted on its rear bumper. The Caddy pulled up at the entrance to the inn and parked just in front of an aging "For Sale" sign.

The Colonel shinnied down the tree, hurried inside the inn, and took up his position behind the hotel desk to greet the happy couple. He was very excited, for these June honeymooners would be the first guests to stay at the Huntsman's Inn in a very long time. The Huntsman's Inn had two things against it – it was run down and far off the beaten path. Colonel Alfton Harris, retired auctioneer, and hence honorary Colonel, had built the supposed replica of an authentic English country inn years ago on the quiet Florida road with the idea that his relatives from England would be comfortable if they ever came to visit.

They never came to visit.

If they had come, they would have found many peculiarities. They would have found the hot water spigots on the right, the cold water spigots on the left. They would have found the table set with forks on the right, knives and spoons on the left. This because the Colonel knew that in England they drive on the left side of the road. They would also have found that the walls were covered completely, with hundreds of photographs, all of them of birds.

The Colonel watched through the window as the happy couple jumped from their car, bounded up the steps, and whooshed through the front door of the Huntsman's Inn, singing and whistling the tune: "You Are My Special Angel".

If appearances counted for anything, Frederick and Petula had it made. They were not young, and it was a second marriage for both of them. But if anybody could be over fifty and still be a "hot" couple, they were it. Frederick was a guy with a big chest, big arms, and because of his curls, big hair. Petula was a tall woman - slender, shapely, well-dressed, and perfectly lovely from a distance - though close up you would see a wine stain birth mark circling her left eye which make-up could never quite erase.

As they approached the desk to sign the guest book, the couple was so excited they hardly noticed the Colonel, though he was quite a sight in his quasi-military uniform, complete with epaulets and tricorn hat. He was solicitous to a fault. He offered the pen and the guest book with a flourish, and with a sweeping gesture, grabbed a bellman's cap from the hat tree with one hand, hanging the tricorn in its place with the other. He set the cap on his balding head, and dashed gamely for the luggage. He started for the stairs. Then, at the foot of the stairs, he began to wobble under the weight of the oversized load - for he was loaded with liquor as well as luggage.

Frederick came gallantly to the rescue, taking the suitcases from his hands, and sitting the old man down on the stair to catch his breath.

Petula also caught his breath, and took a long step backward from the sour smell of English Brandy.

"Just sit there for a little while, ol' Buddy, said Frederick. "Don't worry about them satchels, I got 'em."

"Oh, thank you sir. I am sorry" answered the Colonel,

between breaths.

"You just stay here for a few minutes with the Colonel, Petey, whilst I run up to the suite with our stuff," said Frederick.

She hated being called Petey.

"That won't be necessary, Frederick," she quickly replied.

"Yeah it is, Petey. I know this is our honeymoon, but you're gonna want to wear some of these clothes sometimes, aren't ya?" he said with a grin, as he hoisted the baggage and started up the stairs.

Petula had meant to say it would not be necessary for her to stay with the Colonel. After all, he was a grown man, and could take care of himself, couldn't he? Besides, his reeking breath told her he was an alcoholic, and she despised that in a man.

She moved away from the Colonel as far as she could, and feigned interest in the photographs on the wall. "My, Colonel, did you take all these pictures?" asked Petula.

"Yes, Milady" answered the Colonel, reaching for the banister and pulling himself to his feet.

"Well, the local birds have really provided you with quite a hobby," she said.

"It's a bit more than a hobby to me; you see when you haven't a family of your own, you take a great interest in your neighbors," he said, stepping too close to Petula. "I've always been attracted to birds," he continued, still breathing hard.

Petula pulled away from the Colonel in revulsion, knowing full well the implication of the word "bird" to the British; though she sensed that the Colonel's English accent was as dubious as his rank.

Just then Frederick came down the stairs saying, "O.K., I'll make a quick trip to the car for your other things, and then I'll come back down, and carry you up them stairs, Petey!"

"Oh, no Frederick, I'm too excited," said Petula. "And,

besides, I want you to save your strength. I'll go with you now."

"I shall retire to my quarters and take a bit of rest," said the Colonel, with a clumsy bow. "But, should you need anything, anything at all, just ring me."

Once inside the honeymoon suite, Petula felt a wave of fatigue come over her. She spread her coat upon the bed, not wanting to touch the bedspread or the sheets, and told Frederick she would have a quick nap while he showered.

In the minutes before she slept, her mind took her through the past few hectic days. There had been the quick wedding in Connecticut before a Justice of the Peace. Then there had been the drive to Alabama and the wedding reception at the old, ramshackle farm of Zeke and Effie, Frederick's cousins, or as he called them, "kinfolk." Then, the trip to the Huntsman's Inn.

So far, Petula had loathed almost every minute of her marriage. Frederick's kinfolk were the antithesis of everything Petula loved. Petula's life was lived in pursuit of refinement and elegance. Since the death of her first husband, and alcoholic, she had traveled the world in high style, sampling the best in fashion, food and culture until the money from the estate had run out.

Then she met Frederick, who had loved his first wife, and transferred in his widowhood his love to plumbing. He became known as "The Plumbing King". He had made a great deal of money, and at Petula's urging, sold his business. It was Petula's plan that Frederick would now begin to enjoy life by spending a little of his money, traveling the world with her. She called him her "diamond in the rough", and she meant to polish his rough edges. She would show him the delights of her world, and teach him the meaning of civilization from the ground up. Frederick would say he might as well learn about civilization from the ground up, since he already knew plenty about the underground part. Then he would laugh raucously, and Petula's mouth would curl into a half smile. Frederick would kiss her, and sing, "You are my special angel, sent from up above."

Petula had made careful plans, and had booked travel and accommodations for a trip around the world beginning with a cruise leaving from Miami in two days. The Huntsman's Inn had been a blunder in her planning caused by false advertising. She'd found it on the Internet described as: "The Huntsman's Inn-a wonderful way to escape from it all." Now she just wanted to escape from it.

She had fallen into a deep sleep when Frederick jostled her awake. "Petey, c'mere, you gotta see this," he said

"Oh, not now, dear, I just need a moment's peace." she answered.

"This'll just take a minute, I want you to see this, Petey," he insisted.

She pulled herself up and followed the robed, and dripping Frederick into the bathroom.

"Yes", she said, "the old claw-foot bathtub is charming."

"Yeah, but get a load of this, Petey," he said, pointing to the toilet. "This here's the original Crapper. It's what you call your High Tank Pull Chain Toilet. With that tank hangin' there, eight feet above the pot, you get a tremendous flush. That's gravity at work, Petey. That's what I'm talkin' about when I say: there's just one thing a plumber needs to know - it flows downhill."

Petula swallowed hard.

Frederick went on interminably about the toilet, how it was invented by Thomas Crapper, and that's why they call it a crapper. He talked about the pipes, how they were attached, the amount of water pressure, the number of gallons in the tank, and the weight of the tank.

Finally, Petula begged his indulgence, saying she had a splitting headache, and went back to bed where she slept deeply until morning. She awoke to Frederick's singing and humming, and the smell of bacon and eggs frying in the kitchen. She went downstairs, and to her surprise, found

Frederick standing at the stove, spatula in hand, and wearing a dirty old chef's hat and apron.

"Oh, Frederick," she said, "that's the Colonel's job."

"Not anymore, it isn't," he said. "I made the old man an offer on this place last night, and he jumped at it."

"What do you mean, dear?" she asked, feeling shaken. "We've made plans."

"I'm gettin' this place for practically nothin', 'cause I'm lettin' the Colonel stay on here. He won't bother us, Petey. He'll mostly keep to his quarters. He likes to spend time outdoors any ways, with the birds."

Petula was dumb-struck.

"I love the old guy. But, mostly I just love this place and what he's done with it. Where else are you gonna find the original Crapper, unless you go to England? And, now we don't have to go to England, Petey. We don't have to go anywhere."

Frederick continued on about the inn, and how it was close to the kinfolk, "but not too close, if you know what I mean". He declared that the rest of their lives would be a honeymoon, "right here in the love nest."

But Petula heard nothing he was saying. For it was at that exact moment that a vision came into her mind. It was a vision she would never be without for the rest of her life. She pictured Frederick's hand reaching for the handle on the chain, and pulling. She saw the tank coming loose from the wall, eight feet above the pot. She winced as she imagined a sickening thud as the tank landed squarely on Frederick's little bald spot. Then, the quiet trickling of water flowing from the tank, and the blood flowing from...Oh God!

The days went by at the Huntsman's Inn and Frederick just kept puttering and sprucing, and singing "You are my special angel, sent from up above." But Petula wasn't humming along anymore. Frederick never seemed to notice, for now the Colonel would join in with a whistled harmony. He had learned quite well how to whistle from the birds he was constantly photographing.

Petula made the best of the situation, taking over the duties in the kitchen, and doing her best to redecorate it. But, as one-by-one, all the travel bookings she had made were unbooked, she would think: "the man loves the Crapper more than he loves me."

The terrible vision of the falling tank was with her every hour.

On the day the last of her bookings was deleted from her travel agent's computer, Petula took action. Frederick had gone to the hardware store, and the Colonel was nowhere to be found. Petula carried the stepladder up the stairs to the bathroom.

She wrenched the nuts loose from the bolts that held the tank in place. Frederick had recently replaced them, so it was no problem for her to loosen the nuts so that the tank would fall when Frederick pulled the chain. She knew he'd give it a hard yank; he always did everything with gusto. Petula prepared an early supper of red beans and rice, with good old-fashioned Southern-style bread pudding for dessert. Frederick excused himself from the table and went upstairs. Then, with a crash, it was over.

Petula would have gotten off "Scot-free" if the Colonel hadn't turned his photographs over to the police. She didn't know the old birdwatcher was seated in the crotch of a tree just outside the bathroom window. While taking pictures of a hummingbird as it fluttered by, he had inadvertently snapped Petula as she stood on the ladder loosening the nuts.

Newspapers had a field day with the story of Frederick's demise. The headlines read: "Plumbing King Dethrowned","Found Dead In the Head", and "Man Craps Out In Crapper".

Petula was arrested, tried, and sentenced to die in Florida's electric chair, "Old Sparky". On the day of her execution, as the hood was being pulled over her eyes, Petula saw in her mind, for the last time, the vision of Frederick's hand reaching for the handle on the chain, and pulling.

Dean Johnson was born in 1949 in Jamestown, NY, and educated in public schools and colleges of S.U.N.Y, and received an M.A. from Illinois State University. He works as a stand up comedian and actor, and lives in Minneapolis, Minnesota.

Acknowledgements

I wish to thank Sharron Stockhausen, Bobbye Johnson, and Mary Hirsch for their generosity of spirit and support of this project.

Mary Hirsch is one swell gal, as in www.swellgal.com. Author, playwright, and comedian, Mary's success as a scriptwriter for Garrison Keillor's *Prairie Home Companion*, and as an award-winning columnist for *The Minnesota Women's Press*, is secondary in her love of family and friends. She is not only near perfect, but a darn good marksman.

Sharron Stockhausen's expertise as an editor and writer is matched by her loyalty as a friend. She and her husband, Harry, own an exceptional equity publishing house, Expert Publishing Inc. (www.expertpublishinginc.com). Sharron generously donated her time to this project. As a former president of the Twin Cities Sisters in Crime her love of the mystery genre provided much-needed insight during our selection process.

Bobbye Johnson, current President of the Twin Cities Sisters In Crime, has the distinction of holding the position of Director of Development at Penury Press. She accepted the position after being reminded of the *Cheers* episode when Woody asked for a raise and was told it was good that he asked for a raise and not a title. Woody, of course, ended up without a raise, but a very impressive title. Bobbye volunteers her time, networking skills, and wisdom for absolutely no money. But, we have given her a very nifty title.

We wish to thank Pat Frovarp, owner of the popular independent mystery bookstore, *Once Upon A Crime* located in Minneapolis. Pat's support of the local mystery community is legendary. *Once Upon A Crime* is a home to both readers and authors.

We'd also like to thank our volunteer readers and

proofreaders, Doris Ahlberg, Julie Madden, Peter Schneider, and Howard W. Block, Jr. We'd like to thank Gordon Slabaugh of Adventure Publications, Inc. who chased Pat Dennis down in the parking lot to remind her how much he liked the idea of *Who Died In Here*? We offer our heartfelt gratitude to Babs Lakey, of Futures Mysterious Anthology Magazine, who provided credibility and support for the project.

And finally, we'd like to thank the wonderful organizations of Sisters In Crime and The Short Mystery Fiction Society.

The Short Mystery Fiction Society, an email list group with worldwide membership, was created in 1997 as a place for writers, readers, editors and publishers of short Mystery and Crime stories to discuss writing topics and exchange market information. Their online presence provided Penury Press the opportunity of soliciting writers from around the globe. Visit the SMFS Website at www.shortmystery.net/ for more details.

Sisters In Crime is an international organization of writers, readers, booksellers, librarians, agents, editors, reviewers and teachers interested in promoting the work of women mystery writers. Many of the local chapters of Sisters In Crime publicized the call-for-submissions not only to their members but also to many others in the mystery writing community. The Sisters In Crime website is located at www.sistersincrime.org and has a direct link to many of the local chapters' websites.

Available from Penury Press

HOTDISH TO DIE FOR

By

Pat Dennis

A hilarious collection of culinary mystery short stories and 18 hotdish (casserole) recipes. Story titles include "Death by Idaho", "Cabin Fever", "The Elder Hostile", "Hotdish To Die For", "The Lutheran Who Lusted", and "The Maltese Tator Tot". Winner of The Merit Award from The Midwest Independent Publishers Association.

"Always funny and often poignant, *Hotdish To Die For* serves up a healthy helping of stories that are truly Minnesotan in their details and wonderfully universal in their appeal. This is a book to savor. I not only enjoyed it, I've given it as a gift."–William Kent Krueger, author of *The Devil's Bed*, *Purgatory Ridge*, *Boundary Waters*, and *Iron Lake*.

"A wickedly funny collection ...."–*The Minnesota Women's Press*

"This is a fun book with deadly humorous stories. The reading is easy and enjoyable."–*Heartland Reviews*

"Midwesterners in particular will appreciate Dennis' humor, although anyone with a taste for cozy crime collections should like it."–*Deadly Pleasures Magazine*

112 Pages, Paperback, ISBN 0-9676344-0-7, Retail Price $9.95. Available at local bookstores, Amazon.com, and on-line at www.penurypress.com. To order by mail send check or money order for $9.95 per book plus $2.00 shipping and handling to:

Penury Press

P.O. Box 23058

Richfield, MN 55423.

(If Minnesota resident please add Minnesota state sales tax (6.5%)).

Available Spring, 2004

HOTDISH
HAIKU

Combining the subtle beauty of the 3-line Japanese po-
etry art form with a blend of up-home wisdom and humor, **Hotdish Haiku** offers 60 haiku of nature, life and
hotdish, written by sort-of-Zen masters Pat Dennis, Mary
Hirsch, Dean Johnson and others, as well as 30 hotdish
recipes with an oriental flare. Hotdish, known as casse-
roles in warmer, uncivilized climates, is the loved yet hated
cuisine of the upper Midwest. The included hotdish recipes were created with an oriental flare.

Dogs howling at dusk,
Cats chase invisible mice,
Hamburger crumbles
(Mary Hirsch)

Casserole displayed
Gratification delayed
Tongue needs oven mitt
(Dean Johnson)

Snow with rabbit prints
And a few tracks of my own
It's bunny hot dish
(Pat Dennis)

Penury Press
A publisher of Fine Mysteries & Mirth
www.penurypress.com

About Pat Dennis

Pat Dennis is an award-winning humorist, writer and keynote speaker. Her books, HOTDISH TO DIE FOR, and STAND-UP AND DIE were both recipients of the Merit Award from the Midwest Independent Publishers Association. Her short story, "Bronté Rides The Bingo Bus", won First Place in the SASE/Borders Short Fiction Contest. Her 1,000 per-formances include national conventions, corporate events, civic organizations, women's health expos, comedy clubs, television and radio. She has appeared on the same venue with Phyllis Diller, Senator George McGovern and Senator Bob Dole. Her fiction and humor have appeared in such publications such as *Women's World, Minnesota Monthly*, and *The Pioneer Press*. Pat is the Creative Director of Penury Press. She is married to an air traffic controller who goes to work early to get away from the stress.